Peter Parsons was born in London in 1960, where he lived until his late twenties. He has two children and two stepchildren, and now lives with his wife, Tracy, in Frinton on Sea, Essex. This is his first book, which he began following his father's death and from whose chequered WW2 military career, he drew his initial inspiration for this novel.

To my wife, Tracy, who believed in me and bullied and badgered me into writing this story. To Jack, Charlotte, Tom, and Sam, for being around and being interested. To all my friends in England and America, who took time to read the manuscript and provide their feedback and encouragement.

Peter Parsons

THE LAST WISH

AUSTIN MACAULEY PUBLISHERS™

LONDON * CAMBRIDGE * NEW YORK * SHARJAH

A CIP catalogue record for this title is available from the British Library.

ISBN 9781398434738 (Paperback)
ISBN 9781398434745 (Hardback)
ISBN 9781398434769 (ePub e-book)
ISBN 9781398434752 (Audiobook)

www.austinmacauley.com

First Published 2022
Austin Macauley Publishers Ltd®
1 Canada Square
Canary Wharf
London
E14 5AA

Prologue

(Rome 1945)

The green, white and red awnings of Giuseppe's restaurant fidgeted and flapped in a skittish breeze that danced and swirled around the cobbled square. It was chilly for this time of year but it was still early in the day and Giuseppe hoped the afternoon would bring some warmth.

At the centre of the square, a small crowd gathered at the fountain with its prancing winged cherub. Collars turned against the chill, they watched as disciplined lines of green-clad soldiers climbed slowly into the back of heavy green trucks.

To Giuseppe, the cherub's young yet ancient face looked sadder than usual as its large, pigeon-splashed eyes gazed sightlessly down at the upheaval taking place in the square. Perhaps sad not to be the centre of attention, mused Giuseppe whilst looking out from the sanctuary of his restaurant.

The first truck pulled noisily away, the roar of its powerful engine scaring a wave of birds into sudden flight. A heavy blue-grey cloud of noxious diesel fumes momentarily replaced the truck at the front of the line.

Inside the restaurant Giuseppe stood polishing another wineglass and singing softly as the men and machines began to rumble by. "With any luck, things will soon be back to normal." He sighed as he placed the glass upon the shelf above his head. Selecting another glass from the counter, he resumed his polishing whilst turning his attention towards his daughter.

Maria was trying her best to ignore the commotion outside. She did this by concentrating upon her chores, which were to clean and set the tables in preparation for the lunchtime clientele.

Maria was seventeen years old, slim and of average height. She was wearing a pale blue dress that had a delicate floral pattern. The dress was her favourite and she normally saved it for special occasions. It had felt a little tighter than usual when she put it on that morning but nonetheless she liked the way it made the most of her maturing curves. Over the dress was a white apron, which remained spotless regardless of the dangers that morning's duties produced. On her head, she wore a scarf which struggled to contain the tight unruly bundle of her rich dark curls.

Giuseppe smiled fondly at his daughter. Maria was his only child and he absolutely doted upon her. When Giuseppe's wife had died of pneumonia the previous winter, they had both been greatly affected by their loss. However, Maria had suffered worse, and the loss had caused her to withdraw within herself. For months on end, Maria had become a faint shadow of the boisterous and happy girl that Giuseppe loved so much. In fact, her sadness was such that for a time he had believed he would never hear his daughter laugh again or see her face brightened with happiness.

Then, some months earlier, he noticed a change in her and he thanked God that Maria's spirit had returned. But Maria's newfound happiness was interrupted by fits of temper and bouts of deep sadness. These mood swings concerned Giuseppe and he fretted over their cause. It was at this time that he missed his wife the most. Finally, unable to contain his anxiety, he sought help from Father Alberto.

The kindly priest listened intently as Giuseppe relayed his fears for his daughter's wellbeing. Later the same day, Father Alberto spoke at length with Maria and discovering the cause of her condition, he immediately called again upon his worried friend.

"As you suspected, Giuseppe, my old friend, your daughter has an affliction. I'm sorry to have to tell you that she has lost her heart."

"Lost her heart?" Giuseppe did not understand, and his pleading eyes searched the old priest's face for clues.

Smiling benevolently, Father Alberto clapped Giuseppe on the shoulder. "Giuseppe, you old fool," he laughed. "Maria is in love!"

Giuseppe's initial relief at his daughter's wellbeing evaporated when he discovered the object of Maria's adoration was an English soldier. He was furious and demanded that his daughter immediately put an end to the relationship.

Instead, the following day Maria had brought the soldier back to the restaurant and begged her father to meet him. His name was Alfred Harrison and Giuseppe was surprised to see that he was no more than a boy in uniform. When he said as much to Maria, she proudly told him of how Alfredo had lied about his age so he could help finish the war. The judgemental Giuseppe had grunted in response and warned his daughter to beware of self-confessed liars.

Despite his best efforts to the contrary, Giuseppe actually warmed up to the young man quite quickly. Alfred had a nice friendly manner and was enthusiastic in his willingness to help around the restaurant in any way he could. Giuseppe knew this was merely a ploy to be closer to Maria but he was nonetheless grateful for the extra pair of hands, and just so long as he kept a close eye on the two youngsters, he was confident that no harm could come of it. However, he insisted that Alfredo (as they called him) swear on the Bible that he would respect and look after Maria and do nothing that would impinge upon her or her family's honour.

And so, for a time, things settled into a peaceful and happy routine. Alfredo spent his spare time helping around the bistro, with Maria never more than a few feet away and Giuseppe keeping a close watch on both of them. As he watched them, Giuseppe could not deny that his daughter and the young English soldier did seem to fit together like two pieces of the same jigsaw puzzle.

Then one day when Alfredo appeared at the bistro, he was looking sad and full of anxiety. Giuseppe later discovered that the British army would soon be on the move, presumably heading northwards into Austria, and that, of course, meant that Alfredo would be going with them.

At first, Giuseppe had fretted for he feared Maria's old sadness would return. It was with a heavy heart that he watched his daughter and the boy she loved during those final days. He even relaxed his role as chaperone and allowed them some time alone together.

Giuseppe never ceased to be amazed at the fortitude of the young and he suspected the uncertainties of war had given them wisdom and maturity beyond their years. Alfredo and Maria accepted that there was nothing to be done about their situation, and so they simply resolved to get on with things and resume their lives together just as soon as the war was over. Surprisingly simplistic so far as Giuseppe was concerned, but nonetheless a great relief to a father who had convinced himself that he would have a heartbroken teenager to contend with for the foreseeable future.

But now the day of departure had arrived, and Giuseppe noticed that Maria was struggling to maintain the *c'est la vie* attitude she had adopted since learning Alfredo's news. Giuseppe had reasoned with her by telling Maria that the sooner

Alfredo left, the sooner he would return. Maria had bit her lip in an effort to prevent her tears, but she had failed and crumpled miserably into her father's arms.

The tears had now stopped but the atmosphere within the bistro was heavy with poorly disguised sorrow. Giuseppe felt awkward and tried too hard to put a cheery sheen on the events that were unfolding. As for Maria, she said very little and when she did speak her words were stilted.

Returning his gaze to the glass-fronted door, Giuseppe was relieved to see Alfredo heading towards them. He had feared that the boy would be unable to get away to say his farewells.

"Maria. I can see someone coming and I think that he very much wants to see you!"

Her father smiled kindly and as Maria looked up in his direction, Giuseppe nodded towards the glass door through which he could see Alfredo approaching.

Smiling sadly, Maria quickly removed her apron and headscarf and fussed with her hair, deftly replacing a loose curl which had escaped to hang across her face. Giving herself a cursory brushing down, she looked towards her father.

"Well, Papa, do I pass inspection?"

Giuseppe gazed lovingly upon his daughter, his chin sinking into his fat jowls as he quickly inspected the girl standing before him. He could never understand how he had managed to father such an adorable creature, and at times felt so proud of his daughter that he was almost overwhelmed by emotion.

"Bella Maria. One day when this war is over I will take you to Hollywood and you will be a big movie star," he chided gently.

Alfie rapped on the glass door of the closed restaurant and waited with one arm behind his back to hide the flowers he'd brought for Maria. The door opened and Maria stood smartly in front of him looking as beautiful as ever.

"Hello, and how may I help you?" she asked seriously in almost perfect English.

Alfie looked her up and down and smiled. "Well, you can start off by giving me a kiss," he said, and Maria suddenly launched herself at him. Alfie held her tightly in his arms and spun her off the ground. They kissed deeply before he eventually let her down and presented her with the flowers. "I've brought you a bit of a present, Maria."

Maria's eyes dampened as she accepted the proffered bunch of flowers. "Thank you, Alfredo, that's very nice of you." She sniffed at the bouquet. "A farewell gift?" she asked.

Alfie shoved his hands deep into his trouser pockets and he looked around awkwardly. "Look, Maria," he said at last, "I've only got a couple of minutes and there's no easy way to do this."

"No!" she interrupted. "Don't say any more. Just promise me that you will come back."

They stood in silence gazing into each other's eyes. Then Alfie took Maria in his arms again and pulled her close to him, crushing the flowers between their two bodies. "God, I love you, Maria, and there's nothing that's going to stop me from coming back to you. Not even old Adolf himself."

Sniffing back her tears, Maria pulled away from him and dug a small hand into her pocket. "I want you to take this, Alfredo. It is a charm for good luck, and it was given to me by my mother."

He held out his hand and she placed into it a small wooden casket about the size of his thumb. He saw that there was a join in the casket and tested it gently. The casket unscrewed in the centre to reveal a small silver Madonna within. Alfie gazed down at the talisman which looked ancient. "Keep it safe," sniffed Maria, "and it will keep you safe in return."

"I can't take this," Alfie said.

"You must," insisted Maria. "It will stop you getting shot and you can bring it back to me when all the fighting is finished."

He re-joined the small casket and put it in his tunic pocket. He looked at his watch. "I'm sorry, love, but I've got to go right now. I wish there was something that I could give you in return…I know." With that he removed his beret, and pulled from it the flaming grenade cap badge, which he handed to Maria. "I know it's not much but…"

"It's perfect, Alfredo, just perfect."

Maria leant into him and they embraced and kissed for the last time. Alfie backed away from her and his heart almost broke as he saw the tears glistening in her eyes. "I'll be back," he promised as he raised his hand in farewell before turning to break into a heavy booted trot toward the waiting line of green men and trucks.

Chapter 1

(Present Day London)

Tom Harrison's life was becoming a bit of a worry. It was a worry to his ex-wife Helen, who blamed the trauma of her infidelity for the continued absence of anyone meaningful in Tom's life. The longer he remained alone, the more Helen's guilt complex flourished and now she would openly declare (to anyone foolish enough to listen) that she had ruined him for other women.

Tom's life was also a worry for his parents, who complained they never saw enough of him and were convinced he was not taking care of himself. Although separated for many years, his parents still regularly joined forces to harangue their sole offspring about his many shortcomings, both real and perceived.

His work colleagues worried about Tom too. Although Tom had always preferred being left to his own devices, he had nonetheless joined in with office life, especially the social aspects. However, these days he had become remote to the point where he could not even be tempted into the pub on Friday evenings. The quality of his work was also suffering and, like him, had become dull and unenthusiastic.

However, the one who worried most about Tom's life was Tom himself. He was fast approaching forty, he had few friends and those he did have were all settled deep into domestic bliss and therefore, apart from on rare occasions, were, to all intents and purposes, out of bounds. He felt trapped by a job that bored him but which he could not afford to leave and, worst of all, it would soon be the Easter bank holiday weekend and he was alone in his small, rented flat, with no plans and no one to share his time with. In short, he was fed up and feeling lonely and unloved.

Tom slouched in his armchair, gazing sightlessly at the television screen as he pondered his love life (or the lack of it) and the options available to him. Internet dating and chatrooms were both possibilities but although alarmingly close, he hadn't yet reached the stage where he could comfortably promote his few virtues in cyberspace. He decided to put that possibility firmly on the backburner but with the caveat that he might reconsider the possibility again in a week or two if things showed no signs of improvement.

He considered a possible and uncomfortable link between the drought his love life was suffering and the recent breakup of his marriage. This, he almost immediately dismissed with a silent shudder. Even at his lowest ebb. he would rather suffer a slow and painful death than return to the cold comfort that was his marriage to Helen. It still mystified Tom that he'd managed to be married for ten years to a woman he didn't even like.

His musings were interrupted as the telephone suddenly came to life, it's strange warbling ring filling the tiny living room like the song of a demented canary. Thumbing the remote-control button, he switched off the television and made his way to where the telephone perched on its wall-mounted cradle. Placing the handset to his ear, Tom pressed the receive button and readied himself to decline whatever amazing once-in-a-lifetime sales bargain he was about to be offered.

"Hello, is that you, Tom?"

Tom recognised the Glaswegian brogue instantly and was startled that she should be calling him.

"It's your father, he's very ill."

The voice belonged to the woman his father lived with. He guessed that would make her his common-law stepmother.

"They've taken him to the hospital."

Tom and Ruth had never seen eye to eye and although his father had left to set up home with her more than twenty years earlier, Tom still felt some strange animosity towards her. As a result, they rarely spoke and so Tom quickly concluded his father's condition must be very serious for Ruth to call him now.

Ruth gave him the name of the hospital and Tom awkwardly thanked her for relaying the news. There was a silence on the line as both waited for the other to say something more but there was no more to say. Eventually Tom brought the call to an end by thanking Ruth again and cutting off the connection before she could respond.

It was the Wednesday before Good Friday and as Tom waited for the operator to connect him to the Royal London Hospital, he thought back to when he was a child and recalled how much his father had always hated the Easter bank holiday. He would predict that the weather would be bad because it always was and he would urge Tom's mother not to arrange any days out because in the unlikely event it wouldn't be raining then everywhere would be too crowded.

Even at a young age, Tom had been able to see through his father's cover stories. The truth was that he preferred to spend his days off work gassing to his friends and not in the company of his nagging wife and demanding son.

His father's favourite haunt was the George and Vulture in Pitfield Street, and it was here that he and his friends would meet to share stories and wash their words down with pints of bitter.

"I understand that an Alfred Harrison was admitted to your hospital today. I'm his son Tom Harrison, and I'm phoning to inquire into his condition…Yes, I can hold."

When Tom was much younger, there were rare occasions when he would find himself a spectator at one of these gatherings. He would sit silently behind a glass of lemonade and eagerly wait for the topic of conversation to turn to his favourite subject, the war. His father could tell a very good story, especially once his vocal chords had been well lubricated.

One of Tom's favourite stories took place when his father was stationed in Austria. According to Alfie, at the end of the war, the hills surrounding a town called Graz were home to a band of army deserters. In search of food, these renegades had attacked an Allied convoy and during the attack, two of them had been captured.

Tom's father was a driver and one day he received orders to collect a Major Gardner from British army HQ and convey him to a small mountainside village close to where the two renegades were being held. It was the Major's job to collect the prisoners and bring them safely to the British Military Prison, which was also in Graz, where the two would be interrogated before facing a court martial.

Tom's father always made a point of mentioning that Major Gardner was a pipe smoker who rarely removed the pipe from his mouth. Even when speaking, the Major had a tendency to grip the pipe between his teeth and converse much like an amateur ventriloquist.

Anyway, it was a pleasantly warm morning and the two of them set off in a jeep to collect the two prisoners. When they reached the village, they pulled up to its main square and much to his surprise, Alfie was told to amuse himself for a couple of hours whilst the Major continued on foot to collect the prisoners.

So, for a time, Alfie was left to his own devices and these devices soon placed him in a Bierkeller. Knowing his time was limited, Alfie quickly polished off three or four glasses of the deceivingly potent local brew before making his way back to where he had parked the jeep.

By the time Major Gardner returned with two handcuffed prisoners, Alfie was feeling sluggish. He blearily helped settle the two prisoners into the rear seats of the jeep before taking his place behind the steering wheel. The Major eased into the front passenger seat and set about lighting his pipe whilst Alfie gunned the vehicle's engine into life.

It was downhill all the way and Alfie struggled to keep the jeep under control. The journey would have been hazardous enough in normal circumstances, but Alfie's clouded reactions doomed it to disaster. Misjudging a bend, the jeep collided with a stone road marker which caused it to buck violently. The two prisoners in the rear were launched violently from the vehicle and whizzed over the driver's head to disappear into the heavily wooded roadside. The Major had braced his arms against the dashboard in preparation of the impact, but the force of the collision had nonetheless projected his head forward. Unfortunately, the Major's pipe collided with the dashboard and was rammed down his throat.

Tom laughed as his father told of how he'd burnt his fingers when removing the pipe from the throat of the choking Major. "It's nothing to laugh about, son," his father had told him. "I spent a long time in a military prison on account of that."

"Hello, yes, I understand that an Alfred Harrison was admitted to your hospital today. I'm his son, Tom Harrison, and I'm phoning to see how he is…yes, I see…I'll come right away. Thank you."

Chapter 2
(Dublin, Present Day)

The small room was dark and dank and smelt strongly of mould. It contained a crumpled sofa bed, a stained and tired armchair, an ancient television, an equally ancient wardrobe, a dilapidated cooker which looked as if it had never been cleaned and a filthy sink into which water dripped noisily from a leaking tap. A broken window was covered by a grey blanket and the room's only light came from a greasy yellow bulb which dangled tiredly from the centre of a cracked and nicotine-stained ceiling. The faded and in places blackened floral wallpaper offered a faint reminder of 1950s décor.

Two nuns in identical blue wimples and headdresses sat straight-backed and prim upon the edge of the sofa bed. One was slightly built and had sharp aquiline features whereas her sister was heavily built with the blunt hard looks that one would more usually associate with a prize fighter. In the armchair opposite them slouched an elderly and unkempt man who wore nothing but a grubby string vest and bracered black trousers that shone with age. In his cold withered hand, there rested a half-finished bottle of whisky.

"It's hard to believe we sprang from his loins," said the heavily built nun as she nodded in the direction of the slouched man. "I'll never know what possessed our poor sainted mother to get mixed up with such pond life. God rest her soul."

"Do you think he's dead yet, Assumptia?" The slightly built nun asked quietly.

"Well, Magdalene," replied the other rising achingly to her feet. "He hasn't drawn breath for about an hour now and that's generally a good sign of death."

Removing a small mirror from her pocket, Assumptia stepped over to the prone man and placed it at his nose and mouth. After a few moments, she removed the mirror and inspected it for clouding. "Clear as a whistle!" she announced cheerfully before replacing it in her pocket. "Now we'd best take a quick look around before we leave."

Despite her sister's suggestion, Magdalene remained seated as she stared intently at her dead father. "Why do you suppose he wanted us to come here today?" she asked.

"We've not heard hide or hair of him for near on twenty years and then he calls us up out of the blue and summons us to this God forsaken slum."

Magdalene looked from her father to her sister and then back again. "I had almost convinced myself that he never really existed. It would certainly have been better for us if he hadn't. Whenever I pictured our father, I liked to imagine him being clean and respectable, rather like that American actor James…"

"Cagney?" Assumptia offered.

Magdalene gave her sister an irritated glance before her face resumed its usual thoughtful countenance. "Don't be facetious, Assumptia, it doesn't suit you. No, I was thinking of James Stewart. I liked to picture our father as James Stewart, such a lovely man."

"James Cagney would be more appropriate," said Assumptia. "He was always up to no good and running away from the Garda. It wouldn't surprise me if he'd spent the last twenty years behind bars!"

The blunt features of Assumptia's hard face screwed up as she looked down at her father's corpse. Her expression suggested that someone had smeared a noxious substance under her nose. "When he called the convent, he told me that he wanted to make his peace with the two of us," she said. "He thought he was dying and wanted to put things straight whilst he still had the chance." Assumptia reached down and retrieved the whisky bottle from her father's lifeless hand.

"Well, at least he got that much right," said Magdalene, "and not before time! So, Assumptia, tell me, what was it exactly that you put into his whisky?"

"Least said soonest mended, Maggie," Assumptia responded cheerfully as she made to pour the remnants of the whisky into the sink's plughole but changed her mind after the first splash. "I just thought he was on the scrounge and so I told him we were skint."

"I'm surprised he still wanted to see us," said Magdalene.

"He said that money wasn't a problem anymore," Assumptia said as she capped and replaced the bottle under her dead father's arm. Stepping back, she looked at the corpse for a while before nodding approvingly. "It's somehow poetic to leave him holding what he loved the most. One might say he died in the pursuit of happiness."

"Pursuit of delirium is more fitting." Sighing heavily, Magdalene rose to her feet and turned towards the wardrobe. Pulling open its doors, she was confronted by a small selection of worn and tired looking clothes which, like the room, stank of mould. "By the looks of this place, he didn't have two halfpennies to rub together. Anyway, regardless of the way he treated us as kids, I'm still not completely happy about what we've done," she declared to the wardrobe's dark and dank interior. "It's a terrible sin we've committed and after all, he was our father. We'll be damned in hell unless we find absolution."

"I doubt you'll be finding any absolution in that there cupboard," replied Assumptia as she turned to watch her sister's delving. She was about to continue when her attention was grabbed by a small-battered suitcase which sat almost hidden behind the ledge surrounding the wardrobe's top. "Hey Maggie, let's take a look at that case up there," she said bringing the target of her search to Magdalene's attention with a nod of her large head.

The case was heavier than it had at first appeared and it took both sisters to manoeuvre it on to the sofa bed. "That's not been up there too long," Assumptia concluded, "there's no dust."

Initially it seemed that the case's locks were jammed shut but Assumptia's strength and determination prevailed and after a few moments, they sprang open. Magdalene stood watching over her sister's shoulder as Assumptia took the lid in both hands and slowly raised it to reveal the contents of the case.

Magdalene hadn't realised that she'd been holding her breath, but this was now released in a long whistle as she gazed down upon a suitcase crammed with bundle upon bundle of tightly wrapped banknotes. "Oh my God, Assumptia, would you just look at that!" She breathed reverently. "Where on earth did he get all that money from?"

Poking from the sleeve of the lid's interior was a page from a newspaper which Assumptia now removed and opened across the top of the banknotes. The headline read;

Armed Gunman Escapes with 5,000,000 Euros.

"Well," Assumptia replied as she slowly closed the suitcase lid to hide the newspaper and the tightly packed bundles of money. "That's not our concern, is it, Maggie?" Straightening, Assumptia took the handle of the case in one of her large beefy hands and made to leave the room. "Come on, Maggie, it's time we left."

"But where should we go now?" Magdalene asked.

"Where's the best place in the Catholic world to find absolution?" Assumptia said as she pulled the small case tightly to her chest as if fearful it would be snatched away.

Magdalene looked thoughtful for just a few moments before announcing, "Why, that would be Rome, of course."

"Well done, Maggie, my dear, you've just answered your own question."

With that, Assumptia led Magdalene out of the basement room and up a flight of grimy steps into a dark and damp Dublin night. Linking arms, they quickly set off through the drizzle.

A man sat watching from a parked car on the opposite side of the road. As soon as he saw the nuns leave, he climbed stiffly from the vehicle and made his way to the steps leading down to the basement flat. He pulled a key from his pocket and used this to open the door. "Jesus, Paddy, I never thought those two were ever going to leave," he announced as he stepped into the room. "I didn't think you gave a shit about religion."

He rolled his eyes when he saw Paddy slouched in his armchair with a half-finished bottle of whisky tucked under his arm. "Don't tell me you're pissed again." He made his way over to the chair. "Wake up, Paddy!" he said loudly as he stooped forward to give the old man a shake. "I've come for my money, just tell me where it is and I'll leave you in peace!" He stopped as Paddy's lifeless body fell limply from the chair.

Allowing the body to fall unhindered to the floor, the man looked dispassionately down at the corpse. "You know how to pick your times, Paddy, I'll give you that much." Turning his attention away from the corpse, the man began to search the room, calmly at first but becoming ever more frantic as he failed to find the object of his search.

The sofa bed was pitched on its side and the wardrobe sent crashing across it. Stepping angrily across to Paddy's body, the man grabbed two fistfuls of string vest and hauled the corpse close to his face. "Now tell me, you old bastard, where the feck is my money!"

It was then that the man remembered the two nuns and the suitcase they carried when they left. Realisation dawned as he released his grip on the corpse.

Picking up and opening the whisky bottle, he took a long swig before wiping his stubbled mouth with the sleeve of his black leather coat.

"Five years I spent in a cell with you, Paddy Malone. Every day I had to suffer your bloody moaning and whinging. Nothing worth a fart ever came out of your mouth except that one time you told some cockamamie story about your two daughters both being nuns at St Mary's."

The man helped himself to another long swig of the whisky bottle and when he finished swallowing, he slowly began to laugh.

"Watch out, St Mary's, Connor O'Connor is on his way!"

Connor left the room and made his way up the stairs but was forced to lean against the damped wall as the world suddenly spun on its axis and his vision blurred. He still held the bottle of whisky which he now lifted to his face as he tried hard to focus on the label. The bottle fell from his hand to smash loudly on the steps where Connor followed shortly after. Gazing upwards at the unfocused orange blush of a streetlight Connor's last breath flowed out of his body with his final words drifting on it like flotsam. "Fecking strong brew you have, Paddy."

Chapter 3

Corruption (Rome, Present Day)

Luigi's restaurant stood on one corner of a large, cobbled square. It was a chic and well-run establishment where those who had money liked to be seen rubbing shoulders with screen celebrities, soccer stars and politicians.

At the centre of the square, there was an ornate stone fountain with a prancing winged cherub. The cherub's large and pigeon splashed eyes gazed sightlessly down as long and luxurious limousines deposited their glitzy cargoes upon the roped red carpet leading to Luigi's front door.

Inside, Luigi Pesto surveyed his restaurant with pride. It was midweek and the weather was poor but despite this, he had a full house and the place was buzzing. It was especially gratifying to Senor Pesto that despite initial funding from his more illicit activities, the restaurant was for all intents and purposes a legitimate enterprise as well as being a great success.

Upon a raised dais situated at one end of the restaurant's main seating area, Luigi Pesto sat at his own table (which was never ever utilised by anyone other than Luigi Pesto and his own personal guests) and looked down magnanimously upon his patrons.

Luigi enjoyed his food and upon the crisp white tablecloth, there sat a large tureen upon which was laid a beautifully dressed and presented lobster. Next to this, a bottle of Bollinger chilled in a silver ice bucket. He not only regularly ate in his own restaurant, but it was from here that he sometimes conducted his various business affairs. Tonight, he planned to do both.

Luigi was extremely fastidious. He dressed sharply and everything he wore from his dark suits to his silk shirts and shiny black shoes was bespoke for Luigi Pesto and no one else. Despite his advancing years and expanding waistline, Senor Pesto was nonetheless impressive to look upon and he exuded affluence and power.

Sharing his table was his nephew, Franco Pesto. Franco was the flip side of the Pesto coin and unfortunately for Luigi, the nearest thing that he had to a son. Franco could spend a whole day in the bath and come out still looking grubby. His hair was always lank, and he always looked unshaven even when he wasn't. Luigi spent a fortune in trying to improve the young man's appearance and image but had failed miserably, for Franco still looked a mess even when donned in the most expensive and fashionable of clothes. Sadly, Franco was born to be a scruffy weasel of a man and although, following his late elder brother's sudden and violent death, Luigi had tried patiently to bond with the boy; it was becoming increasingly difficult for him to hide his true feelings of irritation and embarrassment.

"Business acumen, that's what's required to make a place like this a success, Franco. It's not all about making a quick killing, some things need to be nurtured, they don't just happen overnight."

Franco looked downcast and bored. He couldn't understand why his uncle wasn't as enthusiastic about his plans as he was. Franco's friend, Little Lui, had landed a job as a car park attendant. It was not one of those new and fancy car parks but an area of cleared land upon which local authority approval was still awaited for its planned redevelopment. It was an easy job, just checking-in the vehicles, receiving payment for parking and also offering a carwash and valet service.

Then one day when it was quiet, Little Lui and Franco had played some football in the car park. Franco had kicked the ball to a far and seldom used corner of the car park and when Little Lui had run to retrieve it, he had suddenly disappeared down a hole in the ground! Upon investigation, it became apparent that Little Lui had fallen into the cellar of a building that no longer existed. Upon further investigation, it was found that the cellar was situated directly opposite the strong room of the Rialto Diamond Workshop. All that was required was some small pre-financing by Luigi Pesto, and Franco could obtain the men and materials necessary to undertake the construction of a tunnel between the newly discovered cellar and its more affluent neighbour, and this would enable him to relieve the Rialto Diamond Workshop of its stock.

"I know, uncle," responded Franco. "But it's just there for the taking. It couldn't be easier if it was gift wrapped."

"I'm sure you're right, Franco, but just let me sleep on it." With that, Luigi made a grab for the lobster and began to tear it apart with his bare hands. A loud crack signalled Luigi's success and he lifted the large claw to his mouth and began to suck greedily at the flesh within.

Meanwhile, imagining the index and middle finger of his right hand were the legs of a footballer, Franco deftly manoeuvred a cherry tomato around the remnants of his salad.

"Don't play with your food," Luigi grunted through a mouthful of lobster. "It's not good table manners."

As Luigi reprimanded him, Franco noticed a lobster meat projectile as it flew from his uncle's mouth to land upon the lapel of his dinner jacket. Grimacing, he brushed away the offending particle and, in doing so, smeared his lapel with salad dressing picked up during his brief game of tomato football.

"Jesus Christ!" Luigi cursed. "What is wrong with you, boy? Shall I ask your Aunt Sophia to buy you a bib?"

"Where is Aunt Sophia tonight?" Franco asked as he dabbed away at the ever-increasing stain with his napkin.

"She stayed home, said she wasn't feeling too good and so was planning to get an early night."

"Is Tony Lambretta planning on getting an early night too?" Franco tried to sound innocent but knew his comment would vex his uncle, who couldn't completely hide his discomfort at the obvious affection his wife showed their bodyguard and chauffeur.

"And just what do you mean by that, you little turd?" Luigi spluttered angrily.

"Hey, uncle," said Franco quickly changing the subject. "Look who just walked in, it's Luca Casaraghi and his Frenchy eye candy."

Luigi turned his glare from his nephew towards the restaurant's main entrance. Quickly dropping a lobster claw, he brought a crisp white napkin to his mouth. As he dabbed his face, he eyed the tall predator of a man that had just entered his restaurant. The man was wearing a black jacket over a collarless shirt of the same colour. His trousers were also black as were his shoes. To add to the sinister look that this visitor was obviously trying to promote, his dark hair was gelled back in a style that Luigi more readily associated with vampire movies than diners in his restaurant.

The girl on the man's arm was a different matter entirely. She was day to his night and radiated light and elegance. Although of average height, her full breasted slenderness made her appear taller. She had dark blond hair, which was pulled back tightly, sparkling blue catlike eyes and full sensuous red lips. She wore a long white well-made dress that exposed one of her lightly tanned shoulders, and a white pearl choker that showed her neck to be long and pleasing to the eye. Giving his mouth a quick wipe, Luigi raised a hand to beckon Luca Casaraghi to his table. Luca saw the gesture but first steered his partner towards the table that was being indicated for them by the waiter. Once the young woman was seated, Luca whispered into her ear before turning and making his way towards Luigi's dais.

Luigi heaved himself to his feet and held out a hand in welcome to the newcomer. Franco also stood and waited in the background. "Detective Sergeant Casaraghi," Luigi proclaimed. "What a pleasure it is to see you here in my humble establishment."

Luca took the proffered hand and the two men embraced. As they held each other closely, Luigi deftly slipped a thick brown envelope into the inside pocket of Luca's jacket. "It's good to have you on the payroll," he whispered into the policeman's ear.

Luca pulled away and looked coldly into Luigi's eyes. "I'm honoured to be of service," he replied.

"Would you and your beautiful guest care to join us?" Luigi offered smilingly.

Luca was about to accept when he noticed the wolfish leer that had spread across Franco's face as he gazed towards Luca's guest.

"If you will excuse me, Senor Pesto," said Luca, "Isabelle and I have some delicate personal issues to discuss tonight. Thank you for your generosity and perhaps we may take you up on your kind offer some other time."

Luigi took Luca's proffered hand and shook it warmly. "I don't blame you. If I were fortunate to have such a woman, I would want to keep her all to myself, too."

"Me too," said Franco as he offered Luca his hand, which was glanced at but otherwise ignored.

Luca stopped directly in front of Franco and looked coldly down into his upturned eyes. "Tell me…Franco, do you believe in fate?"

Franco felt the small hairs at the back of his neck bristle in trepidation as suddenly he became the rabbit trapped in Luca's headlamps. "I guess so," he gulped nervously.

"Good, that is wise," Luca said menacingly, "because something tells me, we shall meet again very soon, Franco, just you and I."

With that, Luca turned away leaving Franco looking bewildered. "I don't think he likes me," he said as his eyes followed Luca back to his companion.

"That makes at least two of us," Luigi replied tersely before returning to his lobster.

Chapter 4

Confession (Rome, 1945)

Maria Capretti and her father, Giuseppe, lived in an apartment situated above the family restaurant. The apartment had two bedrooms, a kitchen, a bathroom, a lavatory and a main room, which were all connected by a long hallway that commenced at the top of the stairs that led down to the restaurant and ended at the door to the main living room and kitchen.

It was very late, and the restaurant had already been closed for some hours. Normally, both Maria and her father would have long since retired to their beds, but this was no normal night. Outside heavy winds violently lashed a relentless rain against the shuttered windows, which sporadically rattled and creaked in protest.

Giuseppe and his daughter sat at opposite sides of a small square table, its white lace cover flickering eerily in the small glimmer of the room's only light which was afforded by a now guttering candle at its centre. Giuseppe sat with his hands clasped together as if in prayer and his head bowed. Maria hugged herself seemingly to keep warm within the room's cold silence.

Daring to break the spell, it took all of Maria's remaining courage to put voice to her prayers. "Please, Papa," she begged. "Speak to me. Say something, please." Her voice sounded dull and useless. Confessing her condition to her father had been the hardest thing that Maria had ever done. She knew it would break his heart, but she could not hide the secret anymore. Her clothes had become tight and there was the sickness which was getting increasingly difficult to find excuses for.

"What would you like me to say, Maria?" Giuseppe asked tiredly as he lifted his head to look sadly at his daughter's flickering image. "I miss your mother; she would know better how to deal with this…maybe she would understand you better. I cannot, I try but I cannot. Look at yourself, Maria, look in the mirror!"

With that, Giuseppe raised himself to his feet and moved across the darkened room to where a small ornate mirror sat on the wall. Lifting this from its mounting, he returned to the table and held the mirror in front of Maria's face. "Tell me what you see, Maria?" he demanded.

Maria looked up at her father, her eyes pleading with him.

"You don't know what you see?" Giuseppe continued. "I tell you what I see when I look at you, shall I? I see a little girl...my little girl. Maria, you think you are a woman already but you are not. You have your whole life in front of you. Dreams, Maria, such dreams, such plans and now you throw it all away on this English soldier! He is not worth it, Maria! You deserve so much more..."

As she watched her father's emotions swing from despair to anger and back, Maria knew that there was nothing she could possibly say or do to repair the damage and hurt that she had caused the man she loved more than anyone else in the whole world. "I'm sorry, Papa. I know that in your eyes, I have sinned, but I love Alfredo and even if I never see him again, I will love the child he has put inside of me. And one day, Papa, you will love that child, too."

Giuseppe felt more tired than he had ever felt before in his entire life. Tired, defeated and beaten. When his wife lay dying in his arms, she had made him promise to always take care of their daughter and to never fail her, no matter what. He had already failed his wife in this task by allowing Maria to run free and get herself pregnant by the English soldier. Now he must do what he could to make up for his neglect and protect his daughter and her unborn child.

Leaving the mirror to fall onto the table, Giuseppe took his daughter's hands and lifted her slowly to her feet and the two of them embraced. Comforted in her father's arms, Maria found some fresh tears to shed and her body shook and trembled with her sobs. Her father rocked her gently, as if she were still a baby. "Do not cry, bambina," he soothed quietly as he patted her gently on the back. "It's time for you to rest now and tomorrow we can think some more about what we should do."

Chapter 5

(London, Present Day)

The hospital dated back to Victorian times and looked out over the grimy east London streets that had once been the haunt of Jack the Ripper and in more recent years, the infamous Kray twins.

Tom seldom visited Whitechapel but when he did, the weather was always grey and damp. Today was no exception and as he searched the busy streets for somewhere to park his car, he felt his mood darken with each thump of the car's ceaseless wiper blades.

The narrow streets at the back of the hospital were choked with slow moving traffic and just as Tom was about to resign himself to a distant parking spot and a long and wet walk back to the hospital, a woman in a trench coat darted in front of his car and into a vehicle parked immediately in front of him. He only had to wait a few moments for the woman and her vehicle to vacate the convenient space before he could replace her. His good fortune lightened his mood and stepping out into the rain, he made the short walk to the hospital even shorter by breaking into a run.

Tom eventually found his father in the Martha Ward. He was in a large recess which housed six beds, three on each side. Alfie's was the last bed on the right, next to a window which looked down at Whitechapel market.

When Tom arrived, his father was sitting up in bed and looking quite alert. Any momentary relief Tom may have felt at finding his father seemingly on the mend soon vanished as he stepped closer to the bed. Two tired and yellowed eyes turned to him from behind the plastic oxygen mask that covered Aflie's emaciated and shockingly shrunken head. The mask was held in place by an elasticised strap that passed over the top of two enormous looking ears. Strangely, Tom could not break his attention from the enormity of his father's ears and he stood staring at them for several seconds before gathering his wits.

"Hello, Dad," he said as cheerily as he could, "you're looking well."

Alfie stared dully at his son. "I must be dying if you've come to see me," he announced breathlessly.

Tom made his way around to the chair that was situated between the bed and the windowed wall. "We're all dying, Dad," he replied whilst delving into the carrier bag he'd brought with him. "I've brought you the usual hospital rations, fruit, orange squash and that sort of thing. If there's anything else that you'd like, then just let me know and I'll pop out and get it."

Alfie's breathing was laboured and painful but he managed a smile for his son. "You're a good boy, you are, Tom. I see you noticed the ears. I never thought I'd end my days resembling the FA Cup! Why do you suppose they've grown so big? I blame the drugs they give you in these places."

Tom was about to explain that it was more to do with his father's head shrinking then it was his ears growing but then decided against it.

"It'll be all right, Dad, as soon as they discharge you, your ears will return to their normal size. Mind you, they must come in handy; I bet you can hear a pin drop?"

"Pardon," wheezed Alfie and Tom was just about to repeat his jest when he saw the smile that was creasing his dad's features. "Got you there, didn't I, son?"

Just then a pretty nurse appeared and set about checking the readings on the various bits of hospital equipment connected to Tom's ailing father.

"Nina, this is my son, Tom," said Alfie. "He's not as handsome as me but he is single and you could do a lot worse."

Tom reddened and smiled apologetically at the nurse who returned his smiled with not the slightest hint of embarrassment. "Now, come on, Alfredo, you know you are the only one for me so you stop teasing," she replied in an eastern European accent.

Having updated the clipboard at the end of the bed, the nurse moved Alfie slightly forward to allow her to fluff up his pillows. As she did so, she whispered into his ear but not so quietly that Tom could not understand her words.

"Remember, Alfredo, I have the injection ready for you. If things get too bad for you, you just let me know and I will give it to you."

At this, his father's face darkened and he feebly shooed her from the bed. "I don't want your injection!" he croaked suddenly angry.

"OK, Alfredo, but you let me know as soon as your mind is changed." With that, she turned and left the ward.

Tom looked around wide eyed and not believing what he'd just heard. "What was all that about and who the bleeding hell is Alfredo?"

"That name was given to me during the war." Alfie took a deep rattling breath that gurgled away in the pit of his throat. "It was the best time of my life," he continued, "and my biggest regret too. Can you pour me some water, please, son?"

Tom did as he was asked and watched sadly as his father took a few shaky gulps before handing the glass back to him.

"During the war, I spent some time in Italy. Whilst I was out there, I met up with this Italian girl. Her name was Maria Caprietti and she was absolutely lovely."

Alfie's words were punctuated by sharp painful gasps for air that were quickly draining his remaining strength.

"It's all right, Dad, you can tell me some other time when you're feeling a bit better." said Tom who was concerned for his father and thought he would be better off getting some rest rather than spending what strength he had left boasting about his wartime conquests.

"Son," Alfie rasped, "you're not stupid, you know as well as I do that I don't have much time."

Tom's attempted objection was quickly and irritably waved away.

"Just listen. Maria and I loved each other and we planned to get married just as soon as the war was over."

Tom remained silent as he tried to picture his father as a young man in uniform with a beautiful Italian girl hanging on his arm, but the image would not materialise.

"Well, the war moved on and I had to move with it but we made some promises to each other and we meant them too. But all my letters kept coming back unopened.

"I went to see my CO and told him how worried I was that something might have happened to my girl but, of course, he had more important things to worry about than some lovesick private. But I loved her, you see, and so I came up with this plan to go AWOL and nip back to Italy to check that she was OK. It was a bold plan, a bit foolhardy really now that I think back on it but back then it was as if the whole of Europe was on the move. I did not think that anyone would worry too much about one missing soldier especially not since the war in Europe was over by that time. Sadly, a day or two before I was set to have it on my toes,

I got ordered to drive this Intelligence Officer up in the mountains to collect a couple of prisoners. Things didn't go at all as they should have and I ended up in military prison. During that time, I was sent back to England and I finished my sentence over here. Then I was demobbed and the rest as they say is history. I continued writing letters to Maria for a while but gave up in the end. I should have gone to look for her but I never did…"

Alfie's story petered to a close and it was a few moments before Tom realised that he'd lapsed into silence. Patting his father's hand, he said, "That's very sad, Dad, I wonder what ever became of Maria?"

"Well, son," bubbled Alfie. "That's exactly what I want you to find out for me."

Tom stared at his father in open-mouthed disbelief. "Just tell me you're kidding, Dad?" he said in astonishment.

Alfie didn't answer his son but instead manoeuvred himself awkwardly into a lying position. "I'm tired now, Tom." He breathed. "There's everything you need in a biscuit tin that's in my wardrobe at home. Just ask Ruthie, she knows all about it. It'll mean a great deal to me if you do this, son, it really would. I'm going to have a little shut eye now so why don't you go and get a breath of fresh air?" With that, Alfie slipped into unconsciousness.

Tom stayed by his father's side until early evening but Alfie didn't wake up again. Stiff with fatigue, Tom finally abandoned his vigil and set off for home. He would visit Ruth in the morning to collect the intriguing biscuit tin and then return to the hospital to check on his father's condition.

*

Early the next morning, Tom made his way to Hoxton where Ruth and his father shared a small flat overlooking the market. It was Good Friday and so the market was closed and the streets empty except for the large dirty puddles left by the previous day's downpour.

Despite the early hour of his call, Ruth looked no more dishevelled than was usual for her, and whilst formally polite, Tom found her somewhat less than welcoming and he was left standing on her doorstep in the chilly morning damp whilst she went to retrieve the biscuit tin.

Despite having grown up just a stone's throw from where he stood, Tom now felt very much a stranger in his old neighbourhood. Too much murky water had passed under that particular bridge to allow him to feel comfortable. Normally, if in the vicinity, he would make a point of visiting his mother but she was currently away on holiday. Tom had decided not to spoil things for her by conveying news of his father's situation. After all, Tom's mum and dad had been estranged for quite some years now and if his mother carried any kind of a torch for her ex-husband, it was the type that would happily ignite his funeral pyre.

When Ruth reappeared at the front door, Tom was pleased to see that she had managed to find her false teeth. "There you go, Thomas," she said curtly as she presented him with an old biscuit tin. "I guess this is what you're after. There's not much in it, to be honest, just some old letters, photographs and stuff like that. There's no money if that's what you're after."

"Not now there isn't," mumbled Tom wickedly, his subdued resentment of his father's partner spilling over momentarily as he took the proffered tin.

"What was that?" Ruth demanded as she glared at Tom suspiciously.

"I said it's like receiving a present," Tom lied as he turned and bid Ruth goodbye. He heard the door slam angrily behind him as he set off at a slow pace back towards Whitechapel and his father.

*

Given the circumstances, Tom returned to the hospital in strangely high spirits. He welcomed the thought of spending another day with his father and delving through the contents of the biscuit tin with him. As he marched down the corridor towards Martha ward with the tin tucked under his arm, he could feel an unaccustomed spring in his step and an eagerness to again share in his father's memories.

When he reached the ward, he found the curtain was drawn around his father's bed. Feeling some sudden trepidation, Tom stepped slowly forward and gingerly reached out to pull the curtain aside.

Tom looked down numbly upon his dead father.

Struggling to master his emotions, he put down the biscuit tin and took his dad in his arms and rocked him as if he were a baby. He was still holding Alfie when Nina silently appeared and placed a small, delicate hand on his shoulder.

"You should leave him now," she said gently, "I will look after him."

Tom wanted to say something, anything, but the words would not come. He slowly released his embrace and stood beside the bed looking down upon the man he loved but never really knew. Gathering his wits, he picked up the biscuit tin before stepping through the curtain and towards the exit.

"Tom!" Nina called after him. Tom stopped and turned towards the nurse. "Alfredo, your father, before he…before he went, he said that you must find Maria and tell her."

Tom looked into Nina's eyes and was surprised to see the tears that gathered there.

"Tell her what?" He croaked dryly.

"That he still loves her."

With that, a sob escaped Nina's lips but as Tom stepped forward to comfort her, she held up her hand to halt him.

"There's no need. Thank you, Tom, and goodbye." With that, she turned on her heels and disappeared back behind the curtain.

Chapter 6

Departures

Arms linked and each carrying a small, battered suitcase, Holy Sisters Assumptia and Magdalene Malone manoeuvred their way to the front of the check-in queue for the 14:30 flight to Rome.

Seemingly oblivious to the consternation of their fellow travellers and having neatly side-stepped the last remaining obstacle, the Sisters now presented themselves at the check-in.

In her twelve years with Air Ireland, Siobhan O'Driscoll had seen it all from drunken rugby fans to precocious popstars. Indeed, she had manned the desk on the very day that Bill Clinton had arrived to renew his acquaintance with the old country. Sadly however, a strict convent education ensured that nothing made Siobhan O'Driscoll feel as uncomfortable as she did when confronted by the Holy Sisters.

Nonetheless and regardless of their calling, liberties were being taken at her check-in desk, and it was Siobhan's duty to ensure that that did not happen. Taking a deep breath and making a conscious effort to put her discomfiture to one side, she met the crisis head on.

"Sisters, it may have escaped your notice, but the end of the queue is back there and I'd be obliged if you'd join it," said Siobhan in a voice that betrayed more than a hint of the nervousness she felt inside.

Siobhan glanced over the heads of the nuns to the passengers waiting behind hoping to see some support for her cause and was pleased to see what she took to be some nods of approval. However, her words did not seem to register with the nuns who had placed their tickets and passports on the check-in desk and now stood staring at her blankly.

"I'm sorry, ladies, but you will have to join the end of the queue…if you don't mind, it would be a great help," Siobhan persisted, her voice now beginning to betray the true depth of her unease.

The heavily built sister leant close and whispered in Siobhan's direction. "Ach, there'll be no need for that now, you might say we're here on official business."

"Oh, is that right?" said Siobhan as a sceptical eyebrow involuntarily raised itself on her face. "And exactly what manner of Air Ireland business brings you here today?"

To Siobhan's surprise, Sister Assumptia began to wheeze with laughter. "Did you hear that, Maggie? Air Ireland business! Have you ever heard the likes?"

"That I never did." Magdalene casted her eyes heavenward. "Would you please excuse my sister?" said Magdalene with a kind smile for the beset check-in girl. "It's the excitement of our holiday; it has quite addled her brain. However, I would recommend that you do as you are bid and check us in for the flight to Rome without further delay."

"I'm sorry, Sisters, truly I am but I really must insist that you join the end of the queue. There's really no point in arguing with me as I've made up my mind. Rules are rules and Air Ireland operates a first-come first-serve policy as indeed do most other airlines."

Like bath water slowly disappearing down a plughole, Assumptia's laughter drained to a halt. She now turned to Siobhan and gave her a look of such venom that the check-in girl recoiled pathetically.

"Listen, you stuck-up cow, we're off to see the Pope! So, if you know what's good for you, you'll stop fecking us around and get on with your job!"

Siobhan's eyes bulged wide with shock and fear. She would have liked to have protested at the nun's rudeness, to call security, to stand up and leave. In fact, she would have liked to have done anything but what she felt compelled to do.

Tapping her fingers quickly along the computer's keyboard, Siobhan unwittingly executed the fastest check-in in aviation history. "You are in seats 5A and 5B, please proceed immediately to Gate 7. Enjoy your holiday!"

As the two nuns turned and headed off in the direction of passport control, Siobhan let out a long and shaky sigh of relief before turning her attention to her other passengers. Putting on her best cheery face, she tried to compose herself and put the two ghastly sisters out of her mind. The nuns' rudeness had made her so angry, but even more upsetting was her own pathetic inability to stand up for herself.

Forcing her mind back to her work, she greeted the next passenger with a smile and an apology before commencing the routine check-in procedure. A sudden combined sigh from those waiting in her queue lifted Siobhan's head just as an electronic ping-pong introduced an announcement to complement the news that had seconds before appeared on the departure boards.

"WE REGRET TO ANNOUNCE THE DELAY OF FLIGHT AE1073 TO ROME. PLEASE AWAIT FURTHER ANNOUNCEMENTS."

"Good!" exclaimed Siobhan vengefully. "That'll teach the old hags!"

Her glee was immediately replaced by acute embarrassment as she locked eyes with the passenger she was in the midst of checking-in. Smiling awkwardly, she said the only thing she could, "Would sir prefer a window seat?"

Chapter 7

Death Warrant

The early morning weather in Rome was bright and full of spring promise. As for the Romans, for the most part, they remained cautiously well wrapped in layers of chic tailored cloth or fur that would keep them snug even if the temperature were to plunge a further twenty or thirty degrees.

Two men sat on a park bench close to the Villa Borghese. They watched a colourful hot-air balloon take occasional tourists high above the treetops to gaze down upon the city's ancient splendour.

A large black car waited at the park gates. Lounging against one of the vehicle's highly polished doors, a well-dressed and dead-faced chauffeur nonchalantly cleaned his fingernails with the aid of a stiletto. He waited patiently for one of the two men to return. It was not difficult to guess which one he waited for.

On the bench, Luigi Pesto waved away the lit match proffered in Franco's grubby hand. "I always light my own cigars," he said from behind a large Havana. Delving into a deep pocket of his luxurious overcoat, he withdrew a diamond-encrusted cigarette lighter and began to suck greedily on the cigar as the lighter's flame brought it to life.

His attention taken by the gaudy beauty of the cigarette lighter, Franco had forgotten that he still held a burning match. His grubby and unshaven face winced with sudden pain as the match reminded his fingers of its existence.

"Uncle Luigi?" Franco asked nervously as he attempted to wave the sting out of his fingertips. "Is that Tony Lambretta you got as a chauffeur now?" Franco knew his uncle harboured suspicions about the friendship that appeared to be developing between Tony Lambretta and Luigi's wife Sophia and guessed his uncle was keeping Tony exactly where he could see him. He also knew that Luigi would never admit his jealousy and suspicion.

Luigi took another long draw on the Havana before turning to blow a stream of grey smoke straight into Franco's face. He sneered as his nephew coughed and wiped his eyes. Luigi no longer tried to hide the disgust he felt whenever he was reminded that Franco was a close blood relative. "So Tony Lambretta's my chauffeur, what of it?"

Luigi Pesto had never liked his elder brother and he liked his nephew even less. But family was family and since his brother's untimely death, Luigi had attempted to bond with young Franco. The problem was that Franco was an idiot and an embarrassment to the Pesto family name.

"Like father, like son," Luigi would often say to himself. His brother Marco had been an idiot, too, and, as far he was concerned, the best thing that Marco had ever done was to get himself killed during a gangland feud. Marco had been mistakenly identified as Luigi and, as a consequence, had died in a hail of machine gun bullets. Luigi often wished that a similar fate had befallen young Franco. In Luigi's opinion, there was nothing surer to give a man street credibility and respect than an untimely and violent death.

Luigi had occasionally tried to find uses for Franco and had hoped that one day the boy might actually get something right and prove himself worthy of the Pesto name. Soon realising his mistake, Luigi began to hope that someone other than himself would eventually arrange to have Franco killed. Recently however, he'd arrived at the conclusion that he couldn't wait any longer and would have to take care of things himself.

"It's just that, well, isn't Tony Lambretta a bit major league to be a chauffeur? I would have thought he's more used to driving that stiletto of his into some poor sap than he is to driving you around town?" said Franco nervously.

Luigi cuffed Franco around the head. "That's always been your problem, Franco, you don't think. You never think!"

Franco let out a yell and pulled further back along the bench until he was squashed as tight against the steel armrest as was possible and could put no more room between him and his uncle without leaving the bench.

"I wish you'd stop hitting me!" whinged Franco. "It hurts and it's difficult to say anything when you keep hitting me around the head all the time."

Luigi looked sadly at his nephew and sighed. "If your grandmother was alive to see the way you'd turned out, she'd turn in her grave."

Franco gave Luigi a confused look but Luigi continued. "However, Franco, on this occasion, you're right! Tony Lambretta is a big name but let me tell you a story that might even explain to an idiot like you how things work. It goes like this. The Pope is being picked up from the airport."

"The Pope?" Franco asked incredulously.

"Just shut up and listen, Franco!"

Franco quickly raised his hands to the back of his head and cowered, but no blow was forthcoming. Instead, Luigi continued his story.

"Like I said, the Pope is being picked up from the airport. After getting the Pope's luggage loaded into the limo, the driver notices that the Pope is not in the car. Excuse me, Your Holiness, says the driver. Would you please take your seat so we can leave? Well, to tell you the truth, says the Pope. They never let me drive in the Vatican, and I'd really like to drive today."

Luigi sat back and took a long and luxurious puff on his cigar before continuing.

"I'm sorry but I cannot let you do that, says the driver. I'd lose my job! And what if something should happen? Well, it's like this, says the Pope. There might be something extra in it for you.

"And so, reluctantly, the driver gets in the back as the Pope climbs in behind the steering wheel."

"Then what happens, Uncle Luigi?" asked Franco wondering where the story was going.

"Well, you see, Franco, the driver quickly regrets his decision," Luigi continued. "After leaving the airport, the Pontiff puts his foot on the gas and the limo begins to burn rubber. The driver begs the Pope to slow down but the Pope just keeps the pedal to the metal until they hear sirens. The Pope pulls over and rolls down the window as the cop approaches, but the cop takes one look at him, goes back to his motorcycle, and gets on the radio."

"You're shitting me," said Franco, who thought he should say something to prove that he was paying attention and didn't know what else to say.

"Shut the fuck up, Franco!" Luigi admonished before taking another drag of his cigar and resuming the story.

"The cop asks to speak to his chief. The chief gets on the radio and the cop tells him that he's stopped a limo going a hundred and eighty-five. So the chief tells the cop to make a bust. However, the cop tells the chief that he thinks that the guy in the limo is someone really important.

"Well, the chief gets really excited about this news and tells the cop that it's great if he busts someone really important. But the cop tells the chief that it's someone really, really big and important. So the chief asks who have you got there, the mayor? The cop says no, he thinks it's someone bigger than the mayor. So the chief asks who is it then, the Prime Minister? Again, the cop says no, he thinks it's someone bigger.

"Well, asks the chief, who the hell is it? The cop says, I think it's God! The chief thinks the cop is crazy but he asks, what makes you think it's God? And you know what the cop says?" Luigi asked whilst pointing his cigar accusingly in Franco's direction.

"No, uncle, what he say?" Franco replied as he cowered pathetically from the jabbing Havana.

"He says, he says that he thinks it's God because he's got the frigging Pope as a chauffeur!"

Luigi burst into a wheezing laugh, which quickly degenerated into a coughing fit.

Franco made no move to assist his choking uncle but looked on in dumb silence as his uncle's face went from a brilliant red to a deep and dangerous-looking purple. But the coughing eventually slowed to a stop and gradually Luigi's face resumed its natural pallor.

"So, Franco, now you know why I got Big Tony as a chauffeur?" Luigi wheezed and bubbled.

After a lengthy and thoughtful pause, Franco finally ventured; "because Tony's going to be the next Pope?"

The look that crossed Luigi's face left Franco in no doubt that he'd got the answer wrong. Franco might be stupid but he knew danger when he saw it. Quickly backtracking, he held out his hands and smiled openly at his uncle.

"It's a joke, Uncle Luigi, get it?" Franco said quickly. "Big Tony Lambretta, the next Pope, that's funny, isn't it, uncle?" Franco fussed and fidgeted desperately as he prayed that Luigi would accept his cover story and let him off the hook.

"That's very funny, Franco," Luigi said dryly. "Now let's get down to business. I'm a businessman, Franco, and as a businessman, when I invest in something I like to see a return on my investment."

"You're talking about the jewel heist, aren't you, uncle?" Franco guessed nervously.

"Yes, Franco. I'm talking about the money I invested in you and your plan to tunnel into the vaults of the Rialto Diamond Workshop," Luigi said patiently.

"I was expecting a return on that investment, a return in either diamonds or cash. Did I get the return I was expecting, Franco?" Luigi's voice had become hushed and menacing and Franco began to squirm in shaking discomfort. "I asked whether I got the return I was expecting, Franco!"

Luigi Pesto's anger was now undisguised as was Franco's terror. Sitting with both hands tucked between his legs, a wretched Franco wriggled and sobbed at the onslaught.

"No, Uncle Luigi." He sniffed.

"What's that, I didn't hear you, Franco?" Luigi persisted.

Franco sniffed and replied in a louder but trembled voice, "No, Uncle Luigi."

"No, Uncle Luigi," Luigi mimicked cruelly. "Too frigging right, no! I was expecting a million carats in diamonds and what do I get? I'll tell you what I frigging well got, shall I?"

Franco couldn't answer even if he'd wanted to. He just sat next to Luigi on the bench, sobbing and shaking miserably.

"I got a pig and half a frigging cow! Tell me, Franco, what the fuck happened?"

"It wasn't my fault, Uncle Luigi, the plans were wrong. We did the digging like you said but when we broke through, I asks Little Lui, why they keeping pigs in jewellers but he says they must have moved the jewellers and replaced it with a butchers," whinged Franco.

Luigi continued to look at Franco through flint hard eyes and pondered the merits of informing Franco that the plans must have been upside down when he'd set to work tunnelling through the wrong wall. After what seemed like a lifetime to Franco, Luigi softened his gaze and placed a comforting arm around Franco's shoulder.

"OK, Franco, you did your best and that's good enough for me." Luigi sighed wearily.

Something in the tone of his uncle's voice suggested to Franco that he'd finally reached a long struggled-over decision. The icy sensation that suddenly washed over Franco's spine and made him shiver involuntarily should have warned him that the decision reached did not bode well for his long-term survival.

Luigi reached into the inside of his overcoat and pulled out a well-padded brown envelope which he handed to Franco.

"I got another job for you, Franco, and this one's real easy. All you got to do is deliver this envelope. The address is on the front. Hand the envelope to the guy it's addressed to and no one else, you understand?"

Franco felt the kind of elation reserved for the reprieved and could have danced with joy. Instead, he sat nodding enthusiastically, like an eager to please puppy.

"You hand it to him personally and wait for him to give you something back. Do you understand that, Franco?"

"Yes, uncle, you can always depend on me," said Franco as he took the envelope and stuffed it safely into his own pocket. He was pathetically pleased to be given another chance to prove himself and this time he was determined not to let his uncle down.

What Franco didn't know was that he'd just pocketed his own death warrant and the money that would pay for his execution.

Chapter 8

Escape

The door slammed loudly and Luca awoke. Two unfocused and bloodshot eyes opened to see the ceiling turn sharply to the right before readjusting itself. His head started to pound as his tongue attempted to produce some moisture to ease its cracked surface. A wave of nausea caused him to curl into a foetal position until the sensation eased.

As he lay amongst the ruins of his bed, one by one memories of the previous night barged their way into his consciousness like drunken gate-crashers to a private party. Each new memory made him wince and search his alcohol-fuddled mind desperately for something that could possibly justify his actions.

Bracing himself, he manoeuvred into a sitting position and began to cough vigorously. "Isabelle! Bring me some coffee and some pills, I am ill." There was no response. Luca pulled open the drawer of the bedside cabinet from which he produced a crumpled cigarette packet. It was empty so he crushed it in his fist and threw it across the room. It was then that he noticed that his knuckles were red and badly swollen.

Another flashback made him wince again. She must have deserved it but he just couldn't remember why.

"Isabelle! You can stop hiding now, I will not hurt you." Once again, silence was his only response as he got up and reeled towards the bedroom door. "Listen, baby, don't be silly. Come on, come out from wherever you're hiding." He stood in the doorway clutching its frame and breathing like an old and exhausted man. *I really must give this shit up*, he said to himself.

Luca Casaraghi was a fit and healthy thirtysomething with a promising career in Rome's metropolitan police force. Right now, he looked ten years older, felt thirty years older and smelt dead.

"Isabelle, baby, we can work this out," he croaked. "So, OK, I get a little jealous but that's just because I love you so much…come on, Isabelle! I'll buy you something nice and we can forget this ever happened."

Luca began to shamble his way along the apartment's narrow hallway, pushing open doors and checking the rooms for Isabelle as he went.

"Please, Issi, I'm too ill for all of this bullshit."

As he reached the front door, he noticed that the security chain hung loose and that the bolts were pulled back. These were always secured upon his arrival home and never released until he left the next morning.

"Isabelle! You are making me angry again…Isabelle!!! If you've left me, I promise I will find you and when I do, I will kill you, you little French bitch!"

Chapter 9
The Biscuit Tin

Tom stepped out of the hospital and towards his car like a sleepwalker. He fumbled in his pocket for his car keys, not realising he already held them in his other hand. When he finally noticed the keys, he stared dumbly at them for a few moments before returning them to his pocket and turning away from the car to head towards the pub which stood on the opposite side of the road.

The Good Samaritan public house was still empty when Tom arrived, it's dark polished surfaces and subdued lighting offering a peacefulness he usually associated with church. He stood by the door and glanced around wondering whether or not the pub was yet open when, as if by magic, the jukebox suddenly burst into life.

Encouraged, he walked slowly to the bar where he stood with the biscuit tin tucked under his arm and waited patiently for more signs of life. The song playing on the jukebox was *Lucky Man* by the Verve and despite himself, he smiled at the irony. As his father had enjoyed telling him, life was all about timing.

Tom was about to give up and leave when a gothic-looking young woman appeared from somewhere below the bar. She had a small pale face, dark shadowed eyes, blue lips and a mass of black spiky hair. Her Transylvanian appearance was neatly finished off by some small but spiteful-looking silver piercing to her ears and nose.

"I'd like a drink, please," said Tom as he involuntarily locked eyes with a silver skull that dangled invitingly between the young woman's pert and overly exposed breasts. "A pint of lager would be good."

The goth's gaze studied Tom for some moments before she languidly set about supplying his order. With drink in hand, Tom made his way to a table and decided upon one of the burgundy leather bench seats that nestled cosily against the wall and offered a clear view of the bar. Placing his glass upon the table, he turned his attention towards the biscuit tin. The lid of the tin was adorned with pictures of a young but faded Prince Charles and Princess Diana. However, a hot cup had at some stage deprived the young couple of their sheen and now they looked like a haunting premonition of what was to come.

"If you're hungry, there're some hot and cold snacks available at the bar but you're not allowed to bring your own food," the barmaid called belligerently as Tom attempted to lever the lid from the biscuit tin. At first, he couldn't understand what had prompted this outburst but he soon cottoned on.

"Thanks," he replied as the lid finally popped off. "I'll bear that in mind."

Ruth had been right; the biscuit tin did not contain a great deal. A bundle of obviously aged letters had been neatly tied together with red tape. There was an equally old black and white photograph that showed a young girl sitting upon a fence and smiling prettily at the camera. Also, there was a small wooden casket about the size of Tom's thumb. Intrigued by the casket, Tom removed it from the tin and noting the join at its centre, he twisted it open. Inside there was a small silver figure, which upon closer inspection appeared to be a Madonna holding the infant Jesus in her arms. After gazing at this for some moments, Tom resealed the casket and returned it to the biscuit tin. He next took out the bundle of letters and untied the red tape which held them in place. He flicked through them slowly. There were about thirty in all and none of them appeared to have been opened. They were all addressed to the same person, Miss Maria Caprietti. Selecting one of the envelopes at random, Tom replaced the others in the tin before carefully trying to prise the letter open.

"Do you want a knife?"

Tom glanced up from his task to notice that his actions were being carefully scrutinised by the gothic barmaid. "That's very kind, thank you," he replied as she provided him with what looked to be a steak knife.

"It looks very old," the barmaid said with obvious fascination as she sat next to him so she might better witness what was revealed. "Where did you get this lot from?"

Tom gently sliced open the envelope afraid of causing unnecessary damage to it or its contents. "From my dad, they all date back to when he was a soldier in the war. They're all addressed to a sweetheart he had back then."

"Why has he still got them then and why haven't they been opened?" she asked as Tom carefully removed the letter and spread it out on the table in front of him.

"I don't know and I can't ask him as he has passed away," Tom replied patiently as he looked down upon his father's neat script. The barmaid leant close to him and peered eagerly at the letter.

"I love stuff like this," she said. "Old stuff from dead people, it's really cool."

Tom lifted his head to glance incredulously at the young ghoul at his side. "I'd never have guessed," he said sarcastically before returning to the letter.

My dearest Maria,

I do hope this letter manages to get through to you. The others that I've sent have all been returned unopened. With things being as they are, it's hardly surprising that the post isn't being delivered!

Well, I'm in Austria now. On the way here, we came across a prisoner of war camp. Its former inmates were mostly British prisoners and by the time we arrived, they had already taken the place over. They met us on the road and gave us tea and cakes that they'd received from home through the Red Cross.

When we arrived in Austria, we were surrounded by thousands of German soldiers! Don't fret, love, all they wanted to do was surrender to us as they didn't fancy their chances if the Russians were to catch up with them.

Austria is a very beautiful country. We moved into this picturesque valley where a regiment of Cossacks were stationed. These are Russians who, for some reason, decided to fight for the Germans. We had to collect them and send them back home. Of course, they didn't want to go as the Russians will probably execute them as traitors. Many of them took their own lives, it was a horrible job. When they had been cleared out, the valley was full of their horses and so we decided to have some fun. I only got thrown off once but I didn't hurt myself as I was fortunate enough to land on my head!

I'm not sure where we're off to next. Some say Vienna but there's word that we may actually be going to Graz. I'm not sure about Graz as the last I heard, it was still in the Russian sector. Anyway, wherever I end up, I'll be sure to write to you just as soon as I get there.

I hope you're looking after yourself and that you and your dad are both well and happy.

I'm missing you terribly, Maria, and long for the day when I can hold you in my arms again.

All my love,

Alfredo X

PS: That charm you gave me works wonders! I haven't been shot once!!!

Tom suddenly felt a keen sense of loss. Damp-eyed, he stared across the pub's empty interior and in his mind's eye could see his Dad sitting at the bar and raising a glass towards him…"It'll mean a great deal to me if you do this, son, it really would."

Tom tried to swallow the huge tennis ball that had lodged in his throat and tight-lipped, he returned the letter, envelope, and tape to the biscuit tin before closing its lid and standing to leave. Startled, the barmaid looked up at him with a disappointed expression taking centre stage across her pale features. "Aren't you going to open the others?" she asked as Tom edged away from the table with the biscuit tin once more tucked under his arm.

"No," he croaked. "They were never meant to be opened by anyone other than the woman they were addressed to."

The barmaid gave Tom a questioning look and for some reason, he felt obliged to give this strangest of strangers an explanation. "I'm going to try and find the woman that these letters were addressed to."

A look that suggested Tom was completely mad crossed the young woman's face. "Yeah, right, and just how are you going to do that, Sherlock?"

Tom stopped in his tracks and considered this most basic question. "I'll make a start by visiting the address that's on the envelopes and take it from there," he said.

"That sounds exciting," said the barmaid, her face momentarily brightening in a way that reminded Tom of an actress in a silent movie. "Undoubtedly pointless, eventually disappointing and extremely expensive but exciting, nonetheless. Can I come?"

Tom smiled at the barmaid, she might look like a vision from a nightmare, but she had lifted his spirits and he was grateful for that. "I'll come back and tell you how I got on," he promised.

"Whatever," she responded tonelessly as she raised herself from the seat.

For some reason unknown to him, Tom felt put out by the young woman's indifference to his off-handed promise and was compelled to convince her that his words were true, which, of course, they weren't. "Look, I'll come back here afterwards and tell you all about it."

She stood there in front of him looking like the ghost of a St Trinian's sixth former and stared at him uncompromisingly. After a few moments of silence, she appeared to come to a decision. "Name, mobile number and one of those letters…you can have all three back if you keep your promise," she said.

Tom thought about it for just a second before he opened the biscuit tin and took out the letter that he'd already opened. He quickly scribbled his name and number on the envelope and handed it to the young goth. She accepted the letter and smiled mischievously at something secret. "OK, Tom Richard Harrison, you can go now, and I'll see you when you get back. By the way, my name's Zoe," she announced as she held out her hand towards him.

Tom, whose primary actions were never his best, was a bit taken aback by the gesture and didn't know whether she expected him to kiss it or shake it. He decided on a shake. "Ciao, Zoe, missing you already," he joked before turning and leaving the pub and the mischievously smiling Zoe behind him.

Chapter 10
Toilet Humour

On his way home, Tom decided he would leave for Rome that same day, he knew if he didn't leave immediately then he probably never would.

So, he threw some clothes into a holdall, left voice messages for his mother and for his employer, grabbed his passport and set off in the direction of Stansted Airport. Arrangements for his father would have to await his return.

He had prepared himself for a long and uncomfortable wait at the airport and so he was disappointed but not surprised to learn that the first available flight to Rome was not until 07:00 the next morning. He toyed with the idea of returning home, but soon dismissed the thought, preferring instead to remain in the company of his fellow travellers. He decided this was not a good time for him to be alone and so made the most of the airport's meagre entertainments until it quietened down for what promised to be a long night.

Killing time proved to be an expensive business and by the time he was supping an alcoholic nightcap in the airport's bar, he had crammed inside his holdall some new clothes, shoes, aftershave, electric toothbrush, several CDs, CD player and paperback book. He'd actually considered buying a new holdall but decided against it as the lack of free space in his current restricted his spending spree, which he concluded, was no bad thing.

Eventually the shops and restaurants closed, and Tom wandered aimlessly around the sleeping airport, which was littered with thirty or forty other marooned travellers.

Finding himself a convenient place and employing his holdall as a pillow, Tom lay down and hoped that sleep would take him before his mind again turned to his father and the events of the previous twenty-four hours. His sleepy eyes watched a group of young travellers as they settled down amongst their piled rucksacks and he thought gloomily how the airport now resembled a gathering area for orphans.

*

When he awoke, the airport was again stirring into life. He just had time for a quick wash and a shave before checking-in and making his way immediately to the departure gate. He was surprised at just how empty the flight was and a stewardess showed her appreciation for him joining their small compliment of passengers by keeping him liberally supplied with coffee and breakfast baps.

Tom had once heard a story about a marine engineer who was injured whilst working on a shipwreck investigation. The engineer had been part of a team investigating the possible cause of an explosion aboard a cargo ship. The ship had subsequently sunk and was now many fathoms below the sea's surface. The engineer and his colleagues were lowered to the seabed in a high-tech diving bell and this took many hours to safely reach the depth at which the ship now lay. Well, nature called and the engineer had to make use of the diving bell's small lavatory. Having done what needed doing, the engineer then pushed the flush button. However, he did this whilst still sitting bare bummed upon the loo. The toilet's suction extraction mechanism together with the high pressure experienced so far under the water combined not only to remove the waste but also to pull out the poor fellow's innards. What made it worse, if indeed anything could, was that the journey back to the surface and to medical attention also had to take place at a measured pace so as not to inflict that condition known as the 'bends' on the occupants of the bell.

Miraculously the man had survived, but the macabre story of his arduous and pain-filled journey back from below the waves had had a profound effect on Tom who had since developed an irrational fear of using any toilet not solidly placed on terra firma with the benefit of a water-flushing system and a U-bend. As far as Tom was concerned, it was a Thomas Crapper or it was nothing and, as a consequence, he never used aircraft toilets.

This could make long haul flights a bit traumatic and even the shorter European flights were sometimes difficult because as soon as Tom boarded an aircraft, he was acutely aware that as far as he was concerned, there were no toilets. This, of course, immediately made him believe that he needed to go.

Thus, Tom's irrational fear of aircraft toilets, combined with the quantity of coffee he had consumed since the plane's departure from London Stansted, made his first port of call upon arrival at Rome's Ciampino Airport inevitable.

Cursing his stupidity for drinking so much, Tom had spent the last 25 minutes of the flight praying for a strong tail wind and since landing had been searching desperately for a lavatory. The first one he'd found had been closed for maintenance work and now as he made his way desperately across the arrivals hall, his condition had become critical. Noticing a WC sign, he moved as quickly as he could towards it but suddenly found his route was blocked by two determined-looking arm-linked nuns. He made to go around on the left but they moved in the same direction and so he changed his course in an effort to move around their right side, but they, too, altered course and Tom's way remained blocked.

"Excuse me, sir," said one of the nuns in a surprisingly gruff voice, only slightly softened by its Gaelic lilt. "Having spent the night stuck in Dublin Airport, my sister and I, well, we're a wee bit tetchy. So, we were wondering whether you'd ever have the good sense to stop pratting around and get out of the way?"

"Sorry, sisters, but you really must excuse me, it's an emergency!"

With that, he pushed himself through the middle of the pious barrier forcing the nuns to momentarily unlink arms.

"Have you ever known such rudeness, Assumptia?" An astonished Magdalene huffed as she re-linked arms with a glowering Assumptia.

"That I have not, Magdalene. Absolutely disgraceful, and am I right in thinking that that was an Englishman?"

"English, yes, but no English gentlemen and that's for sure."

"Well, it'll be a cold day in hell before Assumptia Malone gets pushed aside by an Englishman and lets the fecker get away with it!"

Pulling her sister along with her, Assumptia made after the retreating Tom.

"Oh, Assumptia," declared Magdalene nervously. "Let's not do anything foolish."

Tom hopped down the stairs to the loo and was racing towards salvation when he was again stopped dead in his tracks. His groan caught the attention of the young cleaning lady and she smartly brought up her mop and gestured for Tom to proceed to the urinals. These were placed directly in front of where the young woman stood. Tom remained rooted in the hope that the cleaning lady would depart until he'd finished but she just seemed confused by his reticence and gestured more vigorously for Tom to get on and do his business. Tom considered a U-turn but doubted he'd be able to make it to an alternative convenience. Stepping forward, Tom assumed the position in front of the urinal, unzipped and tried to relax. Nothing happened and as the seconds passed painfully slowly, Tom could feel two dark Italian eyes boring into his backbone but no matter how hard he tried, there was not a trickle.

"Prego!"

Tom glanced over his shoulder to see the washer woman holding up her arm and tapping her watch meaningfully.

"Pronto!"

"Sorry," apologised Tom. "I'm doing my very best, honestly I am, but it might help if you could look the other way."

In reply, the cleaner pulled a face that clearly showed that she didn't understand a word Tom was saying.

Having a one-way conversation with a complete stranger, a young and not unattractive female one at that, whilst holding his exposed penis was a new experience for Tom and one that he was not enjoying in the slightest.

Quickly changing hands, Tom started waving towards the exit whilst making the type of shooing noise that is universally understood.

The cleaning lady casted her eyes towards the ceiling and turned towards the lavatory's exit but before leaving, she turned on a tap in the toilet full-blast and then marched out bellowing something not too complimentary sounding over her shoulder as she left.

"Welcome to Rome." Tom sighed as at last he was allowed to relieve himself. He had just re-zipped himself when the steel bucket crashed into the back of his head and his world turned black.

"That'll teach him," Assumptia said smugly as she clapped her extremely large hands together as if brushing away dust.

Standing over Tom with her head tilted to one side, Magdalene looked down at the unconscious man at her feet. "It seems like such a waste," she said wistfully.

Assumptia gave her sister a strange look. "I'd say you were sickening for something, Maggie, and if I didn't know you better I'd swear…"

"Assumptia! Now you just stop that right now," Magdalene interrupted harshly. "I'd say we have both spent too much time in this gentlemen's lavatory."

With that, they linked arms turned on their heels and left.

Chapter 11
Memories

The night had brought with it a warm and vivid dream in which she was young again and in the arms of her English soldier. The dream had been so real that when she awoke, Maria was filled with the same sense of loss that she had suffered more than sixty years earlier when she had waved goodbye to her Alfredo.

Maria wiped the tears from her eyes and thought that it was strange that she should have had such a dream. Blaming it on the excitement and rich foods of the previous day, she climbed from her bed and reached for the dressing gown that hung from the peg on the door of her room within the care home.

The day before had been her eightieth birthday and her small family had spent the day fussing around her. The room still bore plenty of evidence of their visit. Cards and gifts now cluttered almost every available surface and the television screen was covered in the smudgy handprints from the younger children. No doubt one of the staff would be along soon to help her tidy things away.

Some of the gifts looked extremely expensive but the ones that pleased her most were those made with great love by the chubby little hands of her great-grandchildren. Cardboard and paper cut, coloured and stuck together with tape. There were dogs, cats and birds. Love hearts, giraffes and paper children. There was also a green paper soldier and as Maria noticed this, she was reminded again of her dream and felt a twinge of deep sadness.

Nonetheless Maria forced a smile as she slowly and stiffly made her way across the room to her dressing table. Lowering herself carefully onto the table's stool, she reached for her jewellery box, lifted the lid and removed the first tier. From the well below, she took a small black velvet bag. Maria placed the paper soldier on to the table before shakily loosening the string of the velvet bag and gently tipping its contents on to the table beside the soldier. Out fell a military cap badge, which Maria now took in her hand. "Royal Fusilier," Maria said in a quiet voice.

She always spoke English when remembering Alfredo, and in recent weeks, her thoughts had turned more and more to the young English soldier that she had fallen so deeply in love with. As she gazed down at the badge in her hand, another tear welled in her eye and fell to splash silently upon the badge. "What happened to you, Alfredo? Why did you not come back to me?" Maria sniffed loudly and patted the tears from her eyes with the cuff of her dressing gown. "When you were taken away, I waited every day for you to come back. What happened to you, Alfredo? What happened?"

Taking the paper soldier and cap badge in her hand, she clutched them close to her chest, and let the bittersweet memories come flooding back.

"We had a bambino, Alfredo, a beautiful little boy and he looked just like you. I named him Alfredo after his papa. You would have been so proud to see him growing but now, like you, he is gone."

"Ah, Maria, what is wrong with you, are you going senile at long last?" She chided herself, the beginnings of a smile once more promising to appear and brighten her aged and yet proud features. "So many years now, Alfredo, and yet you are still making me cry…you should be ashamed."

Just then, there was a tap on the door and Angelina, the young care worker, appeared. "Hello, Maria, did you have a nice day yesterday?" she inquired brightly as she entered the room and immediately began to tidy away the debris of the previous day's events.

"Bellissimo, Angie…bellissimo."

Something in Maria's voice got Angelina's attention and she turned to look at her and was distressed to see Maria had clearly been crying.

"Oh, what's wrong, Maria?" Angelina asked full of concern as she came and knelt beside Maria's chair and took both of her hands in her own.

"It's nothing, my child." Maria answered. "I had a troubled night and now I am very tired."

"In that case, we will have a nice easy day. Are you ready for your breakfast?" Angelina said as she stood and began to help Maria to her feet.

Maria began the slow journey upright with Angelina's aid and had almost made it when she gasped sharply.

"Maria?" Angelina demanded. "What's wrong?"

Maria could not answer and as her legs gave way beneath her. Angelina managed to stop her falling and quickly manoeuvre the old woman into the safety of a waiting armchair. Angelina looked carefully at her aged charge and although Maria had lost consciousness, her pulse and breathing appeared regular. Nonetheless, Angelina was very concerned for Maria's welfare and so she quickly found and pushed the room's emergency button summoning the help of the home's medical staff.

Chapter 12

A Brush with the Law

Franco sped his Vespa scooter through Rome's busy streets and roads. He was making his way home where he would grab a bite to eat and a shower before delivering the package for his uncle. Franco hadn't slept well since the diamond heist had been fouled up. In fact, he hadn't been home since he and Little Lui had blasted their way into Butcher Alessandro's cold room.

Franco had been amazed that his Uncle Luigi had let him off so easily. *Maybe when the great day comes, I'll kill him gently*, he thought as he manoeuvred the Vespa off the main thoroughfare and down a small, cobbled side street. The street had an air of dark neglect about it and the washing lines that crisscrossed above hung like banners for a long-forgotten parade.

Eventually, the street opened up into a cobbled courtyard that was boxed off on all sides by old and echoing tenement buildings with dark flyblown windows and uninviting entranceways. Somewhere, a baby was crying. Here, there was always a baby crying somewhere.

The Vespa's small motor let out a loud scream as Franco momentarily pulled back the throttle to guide the scooter to the tenement on the far side of the courtyard. Just as he accelerated, a car suddenly emerged from a narrow alleyway on his right and stopped directly across Franco's route. He tried to brake but there wasn't enough time and barely slowing the Vespa rammed into the front offside wing of the car, which sent Franco whizzing over its bonnet to land heavily on the cobbles beyond.

Franco lay dazed upon the grimy cobbles but was nonetheless aware of the car door opening and the sound of heavy deliberate footsteps slowly making their way towards him.

Luca Casaraghi squatted down besides the injured Franco and noticed a brown well-padded envelope lying on the ground beside him. Luca picked up the envelope and studied the address before placing it with a smile into his own inside jacket pocket.

"Hey, Franco, I hope you got insurance," Luca said in a conversational tone. "I think you dented my hubcap."

Franco looked up at Luca and his vision swam and blurred before merging the two Lucas into one.

"Shit," groaned Franco. "And I think you've dented my fucking head."

"Now, Franco," Luca chided. "You know that that's no way to speak to an officer of the law. Never mind, on this occasion, I'll put it down to a bang on the head."

With that, Luca pulled back his fist and brought it slamming into Franco's head. Franco screamed and Luca winced as he remembered that his knuckles were still sore from the beating he'd given Isabelle the night before.

Franco tried to raise his arm to cover his head from further damage but his arm wouldn't move. It didn't hurt, not yet anyway but from the angle it was set at, it was obviously broken and there was blood coming from somewhere.

"Mr Casaraghi, I've busted my arm," Franco whined. "You gotta call me an ambulance."

"All in good time, Franco," Luca said soothingly. "But first, I want you to tell me everything you know about frozen meat. Pork, beef, chicken, you know the sort of stuff that you'd find at a butcher shop?"

"I don't know what the fuck you're talking about!" screamed Franco as pain finally started to generate from his arm.

Luca shifted position so that he could bring his knee down onto Franco's broken limb. Franco began to shake and gibber as the pain increased with Luca's application of weight to the injury.

"Please, please stop and I'll tell you," Franco begged.

Luca reverted to his previous position squatting beside Franco and waited.

"OK, it was me," Franco confessed through gasps of pain.

"I know it was you, Franco," Luca responded calmly. "Who else would be stupid enough to use dynamite to rob a butcher? What I want to know is what you are going to do about it?"

Unkempt, agony torn and thoroughly miserable, Franco looked up at his oppressor and was gifted with sudden insight and understanding. "I'll do whatever you want me to do, Mr Casaraghi," he said slowly.

"That's good, Franco, you learn fast," said a smiling Luca. Luca reached into his pocket and brought out a photograph that showed him together with Isabelle sharing a romantic meal together during happier times. "You remember my girl, Issi?"

"Sure, I remember her," said Franco. "I've seen you two together at my uncle's restaurant."

"That's good, Franco, because I want you to find her," said Luca as he shoved the photo into one of Franco's pockets.

"You lost her?"

"That's right, Franco, I lost her," replied Luca patiently. "Now let's get that ambulance before you bleed to death."

Chapter 13

Isabelle Girardet

When Isabelle limped painfully into the Regina Elena Hospital, her story of a slip and fall had been greeted with open scepticism. The nursing staff seemed intent on summoning the police, but Isabelle was so insistent about being a victim of an accident that finally her version of events was reluctantly accepted.

Huddled inside the overly large black winter coat Luca had bought for her, she now sat alone and waited patiently for the results of her X-rays. The painkillers provided by the hospital were working well and so long as she only moved slowly, she could do so without wincing.

Having moved carefully to claim an outdated and much thumbed fashion magazine from a small selection on the table beside her, Isabelle now flicked distractedly through its pages. Her soft blue eyes were blind to the season's-must-have fashion accessories as her mind struggled to escape from the nightmare that had left her battered and bruised.

Shuddering, she remembered Luca towering above her, his fists raining down blows and his feet kicking viciously at her stomach and ribs. She was sure he intended to kill her but the alcohol fuelled violence ended when she feigned unconsciousness.

Although she still found his brutality difficult to comprehend, in hindsight, she might have seen it coming. His actions towards her in the last months had become stifling and she found his constant scrutiny obsessive. His rages had become more commonplace and without justification or reason and recently she found herself watching and checking her every action for fear of upsetting him and making him angry.

He had changed her wardrobe and now all her clothes were dark and staid. Dresses and skirts were replaced by trousers, blouses with pullovers and sandals with sober shoes. He told her how to wear her hair and one day she had returned from work to discover that her makeup had been disposed of.

She had done nothing to encourage Luca's obsessive jealousy, but it had become gradually worse until finally Isabelle had decided that she needed to break free from him. Being as careful as she could not to upset him, she had told Luca that she intended to return to France and stay with her mother for a while. But he had seen through her story and now she sat in a hospital badly beaten and bruised waiting to hear whether or not she was broken too.

Despite her best efforts not to feel pity for herself, Isabelle began to cry again. She had never been treated so badly by anyone before and now she felt very much alone and very frightened. She was in a foreign country with no money, nowhere to live and no clothes other than those she stood up in. She was tired, hungry and beaten black and blue by her psychotic ex-lover. Her ex-lover, who just happened to be a detective in the police force and fully equipped to hunt her down if he so wished. And there was no doubt in Isabelle's mind that Luca so wished.

She tried to sniff back the tears and to concentrate her mind on something, anything rather than the mess she now found herself in but a loud broken sob burst out to signal her failure and fear. Luca scared the hell out of her. She knew beyond any shadow of a doubt what he was capable of just as she knew he would not sit back and let her walk away from him. He would keep her until he got tired of her and then he'd throw her away like a broken toy. It would be when he chose and all she could hope to do was to survive.

The double doors of the waiting room were suddenly pushed open and Isabelle startled in fright. Blinking nervously towards the door, she relaxed when a man in a wheelchair was pushed through and pointed in the direction of the X-ray department. Despite his bandaged head, he was alert enough to give Isabelle a sad look before disappearing behind another set of heavy doors.

*

Tom had regained consciousness in the ambulance. He hadn't a clue what had happened or how he'd got there but a nurse had patiently explained in broken English that he must have slipped and fell in the toilet. She'd asked whether he'd been drinking, and it seemed that despite the early hour, she had already made up her mind as to the probable cause. English, drinking, say no more. Tom was about to become indignant but decided he couldn't be bothered and so instead he submitted to the nurse's unfounded and inaccurate opinion.

The hospital looked efficient and clean and despite an ingrained distrust of foreign medical establishments, Tom begrudgingly noted that it appeared as good if not better than any hospital he'd ever visited in the United Kingdom.

He was now sitting in a wheelchair that was being pushed by a grey-coated orderly. The orderly was about sixty years of age and had a deeply creased gummy face topped with greased back darkly dyed hair. He chatted merrily in Italian to Tom as he steered his chair from doctor to nurse and now to the X-ray department. Passing through what appeared to be a small waiting room, Tom noticed that its only occupant was a young pale-looking woman in a massive black coat. She looked very sad and a number of possible scenarios to account for her anguish flashed through Tom's mind as he was pushed into the X-ray room and the young woman disappeared from sight and mind.

Chapter 14

Meetings

Following his X-ray, Tom was returned to the waiting room. Crouching to face him, the gummy porter tapped his watch and held up five fingers before closing and opening his hand four times. Tom guessed the porter was signifying that he'd return in about twenty minutes and so gave him the thumbs-up sign. The porter nodded smilingly and bid Tom a cheery ciao before disappearing.

Tom was a little embarrassed about being transported around in a wheelchair as he felt fine and there was nothing at all wrong with his legs or balance. He'd tried to explain this to the porter but had failed miserably. He'd just decided to vacate the wheelchair when his attention was taken by the young woman he'd seen earlier on his way to X-ray. She had just returned to the waiting room through doors that were still swinging from the porter's departure.

The way in which she walked suggested that she was protecting the right side of her body and as she sat down, her pretty face crinkled in a grimace of pain. Tom watched as she seemed to quickly become engrossed in a glossy magazine she'd picked up from the table beside her. Suddenly her eyes flicked up towards him but immediately looked away when they found his eyes upon her.

Tom diverted his attention to a painting of St Peter's Square that adorned one of the walls. He checked his watch. It was Saturday and still a few hours until kick-off at home. Chelsea was playing away at Tottenham today and so that should be three points safely in the bag for the Blues. His revelry was short lived as his ears suddenly detected the sound of Isabelle's quiet sobbing.

"Are you OK?" he asked wheeling his chair a little closer to where Isabelle sat. Isabelle glanced at him through tear-washed eyes. It suddenly occurred to Tom that she wouldn't understand what he was saying and so he did what most Englishmen do when faced with a non-English speaker, he spoke louder and slower. "ARE YOU OK?"

Isabelle smiled pathetically and nodded before cuffing some of her tears away. "I'm fine, thank you," she responded in an accented English. "I was a little startled to hear you speaking English. You look Italian."

"And you sound French," Tom responded gently. "Sad but French."

Isabelle sniffed back some more tears and accepted the paper tissue that Tom handed her. She blew her reddened nose and blinked some fresh tears from her eyes before smiling gratefully at Tom who had handed her the remainder of his supply of tissues.

"So why are you here?" she asked him with a quick glance at the bandage that sat comically upon his head. "Did you look the wrong way when crossing the road?"

"My name is Tom," said Tom. "And given time I would have probably looked the wrong way when crossing the road but I didn't even manage to get out of the airport." He raised his eyes and brought a hand up to touch his bandaged head but quickly dropped it again when he saw Isabelle flinch momentarily. "I wasn't...I just don't think my head is badly hurt although I think I can detect a bump the size of...well, it's big."

Isabelle's flinch had spoken volumes and Tom was sensitive enough to notice and to veer his conversation around what he'd guessed was the cause. So he continued as if he'd noticed nothing untoward. "Actually," he said. "My luggage is still at the airport. I wonder what they do with luggage that is not picked up off the carousel."

Just then the doors of the waiting room opened and a woman in a white coat beckoned to Isabelle. She nodded and answered the woman in Italian before turning to Tom and offering him a delicate long fingered hand. "Hello, Tom, my name is Isabelle and I'm very pleased to meet you."

A little surprised by Isabelle's reaction, Tom took her small hand in his and squeezed it gently. "You seem very kind," she said her voice fragile with hurt. Tears once more threaten to escape from her eyes. Tom released her hand and Isabelle turned awkwardly and moved towards where the woman in the white coat stood waiting.

*

Her ribs were badly bruised but Isabelle was relieved to learn that they were not broken. A few days' complete rest and the soreness should go to leave her feeling as good as new, or at least that was what the doctor had promised before telling her that she could now return home.

Home was in France with her family, not here in Rome where she had no one anymore and possessed only what she now stood up in. It was then in a flash of sudden panic she remembered that she'd left her shoulder bag in the waiting room for the X-ray department. That bag contained everything that she'd managed to grab before making her escape from Luca, including her only means of leaving the country and returning to France.

Moving as quickly as her condition allowed, Isabelle desperately made her way back towards the waiting room and prayed that her bag and its contents remained where she'd left them.

She pushed open the door to find that Tom was standing at a window gazing down at the street below. His head was no longer bandaged and he appeared fully engrossed in the vista, so much so that he did not hear her return. In his hand, he held her bag.

"What are you doing with that bag?" Isabelle demanded accusingly. "Give it back, it's mine!"

Startled, Tom turned to face Isabelle and was surprised to see the anger that flashed in her blue eyes. Isabelle moved towards him holding out her hand demandingly. "I noticed that you'd left it," he said defensively whilst handing her the bag. "So I thought I'd look after it until you remembered and returned to collect it."

Isabelle snatched the bag from him and immediately began to delve inside. "My passport!" she exclaimed angrily. "What have you done with my passport?"

Tom watched as Isabelle tipped the contents of the bag onto the floor and began frantically to rummage through the assorted paraphernalia. "*Ce ñ'est pas possible,*" she sobbed. Her eyes full of desperation she looked at Tom and cried. "It's not here, I left it behind and I can't go back there, he will kill me and I'm trapped here." Great racking sobs shook her small frame as she was overcome by her torment.

Feeling deep pity towards her, Tom knelt down and started to put her belongings back in the bag. "Don't worry, Isabelle," he said calmly and hiding his true feelings, which were confused as he tried to absorb the full extent of the situation he was for some reason allowing himself to be pulled into. "We'll think of something." His words seemed to have no effect as Isabelle remained crumpled and sobbing on the floor next to him. "Can you go now?" he asked.

"I'm all finished here so, if you can go too then perhaps we could get a drink and decide what needs to be done to cheer you up." Having replaced all of Isabelle's belonging back into her bag, Tom stood and then helped her to her feet.

Isabelle allowed Tom to raise her and now stood before him in an almost zombie-like trance. Gently Tom took a tissue and dabbed the tears from her cheeks. "Can't have you walking around crying otherwise everyone will think that I've done you a mischief. Before you know it, I'll be behind bars pleading my innocence and no one will be able to understand a single word I'm saying." His efforts were rewarded by a fleeting smile and feeling that things were moving in the right direction, he carefully steered Isabelle towards the exit. "Let's get out of here," he said. "I hate hospitals, they usually make me cry, too."

*

It was turning out to be a busier than usual day in the casualty department of the Regina Elena Hospital. Franco had recently arrived and was now waiting for someone to attend to his arm. At the moment, it was strapped tightly across his chest and despite the painkillers, it still hurt like hell.

To take his mind from the throbbing of his arm, Franco considered the latest twist in his fortunes. Luca Casaraghi had taken the package that his Uncle Luigi had made him promise to deliver personally. Uncle Lui would be very pissed off with him. All things considered, it was fortunate that Luca had broken his arm because at least, that proved Franco was not lying about the package being taken from him under duress. Maybe his uncle would teach Casaraghi a lesson, maybe but somehow Franco doubted that. After all, why go to all the trouble and expense of getting a lawman on the payroll only to have him rubbed out? Perhaps Uncle Luigi would just hurt Luca some but not damage him permanently. Franco sighed, he doubted that too. The only person Uncle Luigi was likely to hurt was Franco and real bad, too.

What Franco needed was a way to get back on-side with his uncle. What he also needed to do was find Luca's French tart. Unless he found her and soon, Luca was going to blow the whistle on him and Franco quivered at the thought of being sent to prison on a charge of breaking and entering a butcher's! Christ, he'd never be able to live that one down.

Franco's unhappy circle of thoughts continued for a short time before his attention began to flit. First he looked leeringly towards a young nurse and tried hard to imagine what she would look like naked. After failing in this, he started to check out the other medical staff and waiting patients but couldn't see any as attractive as the nurse. Eventually his attention drifted towards the two rows of automatic double doors that were the entrance to the casualty unit. An ambulance had just pulled up outside and hospital staff rushed to accept its needy occupant.

His interest suddenly awakened by this small drama, Franco raised himself and drifted towards the doors so that he could get a closer look. The ambulance's occupant was an elderly lady. She looked strangely familiar to Franco and he wondered whether she might be a television personality or movie star of yesteryear. However, try as he might, he couldn't manage to put a name to her.

The orderlies and nurses manoeuvred their patient into the hospital, one nurse marching beside the bed and holding aloft a clear bag of liquid that had been plugged into the old woman's arm. The patient herself appeared in some distress but was nonetheless conscious, her eyes darting about wildly as she pleaded through her oxygen mask to be allowed to return home. A doctor met the procession and enquired into the circumstances.

Reading from a clipboard, an attendant nurse announced, "Maria Caprietti. Aged 80 years. Chest pains, irregular pulse and hyperventilation."

"Maria Caprietti," Franco echoed quietly. "Could be that my luck is changing!"

It was then that Franco saw Isabelle emerge into view side by side with some guy and looking cosy too. "This is just getting better and better," he mumbled to himself excitedly.

Tom noted the emergency unfolding in their path and impulsively taking Isabelle by the arm, he guided them both back against the wall to allow the trolley and medical staff clear access.

As the trolley passed, the old woman fixed her eyes on Tom. He was puzzled by the intensity of the old woman's stare and flinched when she reached out and grabbed a handful of his jacket. With surprising strength, she drew him towards her and he could do nothing but join the procession that surrounded the trolley. As he tried vainly to gently release his jacket from her grip, the old woman began speaking urgently to Tom in Italian.

Isabelle looked as surprised as Tom as she, too, hobbled after the trolley with Franco following close behind.

The assembly stopped when it reached the elevator and it seemed to Tom that all of the medical staff were talking to him at once. Although he couldn't understand a single word, the message was very clear.

"I'm sorry," said Tom. "I'm trying to get out of your way, I really am, but she just won't let go of me!"

At the sound of his voice, Maria became even more agitated and a member of the medical staff struggled to keep her from falling off the trolley, whilst another quickly administered an injection into her arm.

"Alfredo!" Maria cried in English. "Alfredo, I knew you'd come back to me. I love you so much, Alfredo, please don't you leave me again!"

"If you'd just let me have my jacket back, I'd be awfully grateful," Tom begged as he tried to gently prize Maria's fingers open.

It was then that the lift doors opened and simultaneously the relaxant administered to Maria took effect. The old woman continued to gaze at Tom pleadingly as she released him and disappeared together with her attendants into the elevator.

"Do you always have this effect on women?" Isabelle asked as she and Tom watched the lift doors close.

Tom looked at Isabelle and was pleased to see that, although she looked tired and more than a little washed out, she was nonetheless smiling. "We've known each other for about two hours already and you've grabbed nothing but my attention," he said as he smoothed the creases from his jacket.

Isabelle smiled at this and taking Tom's arm, the two-walking wounded turned and once again made their way towards the exit of the hospital. They passed Franco who occupied one of the chairs that stood against both walls of the corridor and pretended to be asleep. Isabelle saw him sitting there and was sure that she'd seen this man somewhere before. This made her feel uncomfortable and when Tom asked if she was OK, Isabelle glanced back over her shoulder but the chair was now empty and the man was nowhere to be seen. "Yes, I'm fine, thank you, Tom," she said distractedly. "But I will be even better just as soon as we get out of here." With that, they turned and left.

*

"Jesus Christ!" Franco gasped. He was sitting in one of the hospital's toilet cubicles and was shaking with excitement. "Jesus fucking Christ! Alfredo Caprietti is back! Oh my God!!!"

"Excuse me, sir. Are you all right in there?"

Chapter 15

Nuns on the Run

Assumptia took the black knob in her beefy hand, turned it clockwise and pushed open the worn and heavy hotel room door. The room behind was dark and smelt of stale cigarette smoke. "Just wait here a second, Magdalene, and I'll open the curtains," said Assumptia as she made her way carefully into the room.

A moment later, there was a crash followed by a curse and a reverberating bong. "I cracked me fecking leg!" Assumptia exclaimed from the darkness within.

"You stay just where you are, Assumptia," Magdalene advised. "And I'll find the light switch."

Magdalene reached out a hand and began to pat the wall close to the doorway. Just a few seconds later, her hand came in contact with the light switch, which clicked on to illuminate the room with a dull yellow light.

"I preferred it when it was dark," Magdalene muttered as she took in the room and its tired and faded décor. Assumptia remained on the bed, red faced and rubbing her knee. "It'll have to do, I suppose," Magdalene continued. "A bit of fresh air and natural light wouldn't go amiss." With that, Magdalene brought the two small cases into the room and closed the door behind them before crossing the room and pulling open the curtains. The window proved challenging but Magdalene prevailed and she eventually managed to pull the sash screeching upwards to be rewarded by a lazy puff of warm air.

"Do you know, Assumptia," said Magdalene turning to look down upon her sister. "We've got the money, more than enough money. So why in heavens name could we not check into somewhere a bit nicer than this? I mean, would you just look at the state of it! It's not been cleaned; this side of the resurrection and the furniture looks like it sailed on the ark with Noah himself! I've spent the last thirty years of my life cooped up in that Spartan prison otherwise known as the Convent of our Blessed Mother Mary only to have it replaced by a gothic dungeon in Rome!"

"Do you think I like it any better than you do, Magdalene?" Assumptia responded as she raised herself from the bed and turned to face her sister. "You've not been alone in that convent for thirty years, have you? No, you haven't because I've been right there by your side and looking out for you. In the circumstances, it would give me great pleasure if you would shut the feck up and show a wee bit of appreciation!"

Magdalene could always be daunted by Assumptia's aggression but gathering herself, she turned to meet her sister squarely on. "There's no need for that kind of language, Assumptia, and you know I don't approve." Over the years, Magdalene had learnt that the moral high ground was a good place to be if and when Assumptia looked as if she might lose her temper. "All I'm saying is that it would have been nice to enjoy a bit of luxury for a change."

"It would have been nice to enjoy a bit of luxury for a change," Assumptia mimicked cruelly. "Have you had your nose stuck so far in the air that it escaped your notice that we happen to be on the run?"

"Now, come on, Assumptia!" Magdalene retorted, her own voice rising in outrage. "I do think you are exaggerating somewhat. I know we did a bad thing. In fact, it is hard for me to think of anything worse than what we did and that is why we have come to Rome in search of forgiveness. But to say that we're on the run! Well, it's just nonsense, that's what it is."

"How so, sister?" Assumptia asked menacingly.

"Simply because no one wants to capture us. No one is aware of what we've done and even when someone eventually stumbles across our father's body, there's very little chance that he'll be associated with us after all of these years."

Assumptia stood silently, considering her sister's response before grunting acknowledgement at the wisdom of her words. "Ach, you could be right, Magdalene, who would guess that Ireland's most wanted would have two daughters devoting their lives to God and more's to the point, who on earth would care?"

The room became heavy with silence as the two sisters stood together alone. "We'll never get to heaven now," said Magdalene sadly, her words sounding somehow alien as they intruded upon the hush.

"Don't you fret now, Maggie," Assumptia said gently as she raised one of her beefy red hands to brush its fingers against Magdalene's soft cheek. "If anyone ever deserved to die, it was him." Magdalene's objection was cut short as Assumptia shushed her and continued. "Think of the way he treated poor Ma, he as good as killed her himself. And what he did to us when she was no longer there to stop him. Think how because of him, we ended up in this home and that home until there was nowhere left for us but the convent. Think how we had to stay hidden away there because of his shenanigans. Think how he robbed and cheated us of a chance to enjoy a proper life. And despite all that, it was he that came looking for us. It was him that wanted to bring more pain and misery upon us." Assumptia's voice was cracking and breaking with emotion and the two sisters held each other closely and wept. Their father had never failed to make them cry.

Pulling out of the embrace, Assumptia cuffed a sleeve across her nose and sniffed loudly. "Actually, I enjoyed killing the old bastard." She leant over and flicked open the locks of her suitcase and lifted the lid to reveal a mass of tightly packed bank notes. "And all that cash he had on him will go some way towards making up for the dog's life he gave us."

Magdalene smiled. "I wish I could see things as clearly as you, Assumptia."

"And I as you," responded Assumptia. "Tomorrow we'll find ourselves a decent hotel. In fact, let's not wait until tomorrow, let's find one right now!"

"Oh, Assumptia, that would be grand, that really would!" Magdalene responded gleefully. "And tomorrow we shall go to the Vatican and see the Pope himself!"

Magdalene was nearly hopping with excitement but her sister stopped dead and looked up at her as though she had gone completely mad. "Don't be soft, Maggie, there's no way we can see the Pope."

"Oh but there is, Assumptia!" Magdalene exclaimed, who was obviously losing her battle to contain her excitement. "Tomorrow is Sunday and every Sunday at 12:00, the Pope addresses the visitors to the Vatican from his balcony! It says so in this here guidebook!"

Assumptia glanced at the green and white pocket guidebook that Magdalene waved before her. "Maggie, what in heavens name are you expecting?" she asked as she again locked eyes with her sister. "The Pope isn't going to stand out on his balcony and say by the way, if Maggie and Assumptia Malone are here today, that's grand because I just wanted to forgive them for murdering their old man."

Magdalene seemed a trifle embarrassed at her sister's brutal summing up of her feelings and hurriedly replaced the guidebook into a pocket of her long dark blue coat. "Well, it can't do any harm now, can it?" she opined. "And besides, I want to pop into St Peter's and say a little prayer of thanks to the Church for taking us in and looking after us for all of those years and."

"And then what, Maggie?" Assumptia interrupted. "Do you want to see if you can borrow a horsehair shirt or maybe even get yourself flogged?"

"No, actually I don't, Assumptia," Magdalene responded calmly. "I want to do some shopping. I want to buy some proper clothes and I want to feel like a real person for once."

Assumptia threw her arms in the air and laughed with delight. "That's my Maggie, now you're talking sense!"

"Thank you, Assumptia, but first I need to go to St Peter's and put my mind and heart at rest. I know you think I'm being foolish but I feel sure that if I pray hard enough that God will give me a sign, in fact, I know he will!"

Chapter 16
Alfredo Caprietti

"Hurry up, Tony, the game's about to start!" Luigi Pesto called from the comfort of his over-stuffed armchair. When Luigi took time off from his various businesses, which was not often, there was nothing he liked more than to take in a good football match. When he was a younger man, he would obtain tickets and join the crowds of other supporters at the stadium but these days he felt vulnerable amongst the tightly packed humanity of the arena. Now he would rather watch the game from the comfort of the small apartment situated above his restaurant.

Tony Lambretta's big frame emerged from the kitchen. He was holding a freshly opened bottle of beer in one hand and a huge sandwich in the other. "It's a nice place you have here, Luigi," he said taking in the elegant 1940s' décor of the room.

"Yeah," Luigi responded absently as he suspiciously eyed Tony's sandwich. "My wife has an eye for detail and she loves all this old shit. Talking about my wife, did she make you that sandwich?"

Tony ignored Luigi's probing question and concentrated instead on the room's elegant if dated charm. "No, it's cool," he insisted. "It's like being on a movie set, *The Godfather* or something like that. I really dig the telephone, my grandmother used to have one just like it."

The telephone sat on a heavy dark oak and green leather topped bureau desk that was situated beneath one of the apartment's sash windows. At a glance, the classic curved solid black telephone looked authentic but the voice box and accompanying button selection unsuccessfully hidden behind a marble statuette of the god Hermes told a very different story.

"That's very interesting," said Luigi in a voice that suggested that he was not in the slightest bit interested in anything that Tony had to say. "Now, if you don't mind, Tony, its Roma verses Lazio and so can we make like two men and enjoy the game or would you prefer to discuss the soft furnishings?"

Tony cleared his throat and made for an armchair. He'd just relaxed and focused upon the television when the telephone rang.

"Jesus fucking Christ!" Luigi cursed. "Is it too much to ask?" He slammed his bottle of beer down on the small dark wood coffee table and raised himself to answer the phone. Stepping over to the leather topped desk, Luigi lifted the telephone's receiver. "Hello?" he breathed unenthusiastically into the mouthpiece.

"Hello, Uncle Luigi!" Franco's voice crackled excitedly in response. "Jesus, have I got some news for you!"

"Franco? Why aren't you de—" Luigi stopped himself just in time. "Why didn't you deliver that package like I asked you to?"

"There's no time to explain that now, uncle," Franco replied before pausing momentarily to wonder how his uncle already knew that the package hadn't been delivered. He quickly decided to sidestep the issue and concentrate upon gaining some kudos with his uncle. "Alfredo Caprietti's back in town."

The news was initially greeted by a stony silence. Eventually Luigi coughed a few times and cleared his throat. "Repeat that, would you, please, Franco?" he asked in polite calmness. "For a second there, I thought you said that Alfredo Caprietti is back in town."

Franco moved away from the telephone's earpiece as it was momentarily filled with Luigi's unconvincingly laughter. He waited a few seconds before once again placing it close to his face. "That's right, uncle, I saw him with my own eyes!"

"Where and how do you know it was Alfredo Caprietti?"

"In the hospital and I know it was him because I heard his mother call to him," Franco replied quickly.

"OK, Franco, now take a deep breath and slow down," Luigi said calmly. "Tell me exactly what you saw and heard. Everything, you got that?"

"Well," Franco began. "I was on my way to deliver that package like you asked me to when I bumped into that bum Casaraghi. Tell you the truth, Uncle Luigi, he bumped into me and real hard too! He broke my frigging arm! Anyway, his girl Isabelle has run out on him. No surprise, do you remember her, uncle? French and really sexy, what I wouldn't give for half an hour in the sack with her."

"Just stick to the story, Franco," Luigi encouraged patiently.

"Well," continued Franco. "He wants me to find her for him and you know what? I found her in the hospital where I was getting my arm fixed."

Franco went on to tell Luigi everything he'd seen and heard at the hospital. When he'd finished recounting that morning's events, the line was silent again. Franco waited and had just concluded that he'd been cut off when Luigi's voice broke the silence.

"OK, Franco, you've done good, real good. Here's what you do next. Stay at the hospital and keep watch on Maria Caprietti. I'll be in contact later but for now, it's down to you. Can I trust you not to screw up, Franco?"

Franco felt elated at the tone of his uncle's voice and the trust that he was placing in him. This was big, really big, and he was Luigi Pesto's man at the sharp end.

"You got it, uncle!" Franco replied enthusiastically.

*

Luigi replaced the telephone receiver and pondered the unexpected news that he'd been given.

"What's up, Luigi?" Tony asked through a mouthful of salami. "Is there a problem?"

Luigi rubbed a large meaty hand over his mouth as he considered what his next move should be. Slowly making his way back over to his armchair, he picked up the remote control for the television and hitting its red button, he turned the set off. Sitting back down, he reclaimed his beer and helped himself to a long guzzle. Turning to Tony Lambretta, who was sitting dumbly in the adjacent armchair, Luigi asked, "Do you remember Alfredo Caprietti?"

"Who?" Tony responded with a confused look on his big flat face.

"Enough said," said Luigi as he adjusted his not insubstantial weight into a more comfortable position. "Before you arrived in Rome."

Luigi looked thoughtful as he carefully arranged the sequences of the Alfredo Caprietti story in his head before continuing. At last satisfied, he began, "Alfredo Caprietti worked for the Titaro family. At that time, we all worked for the Titaro family. They played the music and we all danced."

Tony looked over at Luigi and saw that he had a faraway look in his eyes as though he were peering back through time itself. "Did you dance to the Titaro music, too, Luigi?"

"We all did, Tony, back then the Titaro family was much like the Pesto family is today but bigger, much bigger," Luigi answered. "They controlled everything, gambling, vice, the mayor, everything and their main man was Alfredo Pretty Boy Caprietti. The old Don, Gian Luigi Titaro had been sweet on Caprietti's mother, some said that Alfredo was his bastard. Whether that's true or not, I can't say but what I will tell you is that Don Titaro treated that boy like a son. Like me, the old Don only had daughters and so he came to rely heavily on Caprietti. In fact, he was grooming Caprietti to take over from him one day."

"Can I get you another beer, Luigi?" Tony offered. "And maybe you'd like some salami?"

"And then," Luigi continued oblivious to Tony's interruption. "A bank job went wrong and Caprietti got lifted. For years, the cops had been looking to get their hands on Caprietti and shake up the families but despite all their efforts, nothing. And then, this bank job screws up and he just falls right into their lap. To start off with the cops couldn't get a thing out of him. The old Don he was devastated that his righthand man had been taken and nervous too. He and Caprietti had been holding the other families in an iron grip and many of us believed that by that time Caprietti was the main force within the Titaro family. With him gone, well, things might change. The wolves were moving in and when Caprietti got sentenced to thirty years imprisonment, well, it was only a matter of time."

Tony lifted the lid off another beer bottle and placed it on the coffee table ready should Luigi feel in need of more refreshments.

"But then Caprietti did a deal with the authorities. They let him go and he went into hiding. In exchange, he gave them enough dirt for them to lock up practically every face of any note in the Rome crime racket including his own Don Titaro. The old Don died in prison and so did a few others. The rest have been trying to cut deals ever since. All they do is dish more dirt on each other and all the time their sentences get longer. Honour amongst thieves! There aren't any of those guys ever going to see daylight again."

Luigi paused and reached out to flip the lid of a rosewood cigar box and withdraw a large Havana. Sticking this into his mouth, he reached in his pocket for the diamond encrusted cigarette lighter, which he ignited to momentarily disappear behind a large cloud of blue smoke. "Actually," he continued. "Caprietti did the Pesto family a service. Back then, we were strictly small fry and that's why we escaped the fall out. Then there was no one left in our way and me and my brother Marco, we shot to the top of the pile and I mean that literally. We had some small troubles and Marco went and got himself killed but apart from that, it all worked out just fine."

"So what's the problem now?" Tony asked.

"It looks like Caprietti has decided to come home," Luigi said sadly. "And he probably wants to take my place and that is not a good thing Tony, not good at all."

"Well, Luigi, in that case, we'll just have to make him dead," Tony responded firmly as he plunged the full length of his stiletto into the body of a large salami that moments before he'd pulled from his trouser pocket.

Luigi glanced over at Tony who was now twisting the stiletto's blade slowly but enthusiastically within the salami's body. "That's right, Tony," he responded tiredly. "We'll just have to make him dead…did my wife give you that salami?"

Chapter 17

A Friend in Need

Once outside of the hospital, Tom began to look about him not sure of which direction to take. Isabelle still held on to his arm and to Tom, she didn't look at all well. Her face was almost devoid of colour so much so that even her lips were pale.

"We'd best find somewhere that you can rest and grab a coffee or something," he suggested. "Perhaps you'll perk up a bit if you have something to eat."

Isabelle smiled wanly in response and shook her head negatively. "No, thank you, Tom, I'm not very hungry. My car is not far from here and if you would like, I will take you back to the airport so that you can collect your baggage. It's not very far."

He turned to her and was troubled by what he saw in her face, she really did look washed out and in need of some rest. He decided not to relay his misgivings and instead asked, "Are you sure you're up for that? I can always get a taxi."

She looked at him sadly. "I have nothing better to do right now," she said flatly.

Tom had a caring nature and although his instincts warned him that prolonging his association with Isabelle might lead to all kinds of unwanted trouble, it just wasn't in him to walk away and abandon her. Such an action would have haunted him for some considerable time.

In the past, he'd often found that his conscience and sense of rightness had been a major obstacle to his fun, especially as he grew up in one of the rougher parts of London where such attributes were uncommon. So, sighing inwardly, he allowed himself to be led to where Isabelle had parked her car.

Isabelle directed Tom towards a road crossing. It was similar to a zebra crossing in so much as white stripes had been painted on the tarmac but there were no Belisha beacons. As they approached, he was surprised to see that someone had dumped a tatty and dented old Renault on the crossing itself. Pointing towards the car, Tom wasn't shy in relaying his first impression of Rome's Highway Code to Isabelle.

"This type of thing is not allowed in the United Kingdom," he said. "Of course, some people do dump their old wrecks but I've never before seen one left on a crossing like that. Judging by its condition, it must have been here for ages! Maybe it belonged to Julius Caesar?"

Isabelle stopped and gave Tom a strange look. "If you don't like my car, we can get a taxi to the airport but you must pay."

"That's very good." Tom smiled but his smile soon faded when Isabelle produced a key and opened the driver's side door. "Nice car," he lied as he made his way around to the passenger door. Tom could tell by the difficulty that Isabelle had entering the car that she was in lots of pain. "Are you OK to drive?"

"It's good I drive," she responded. "It helps me to forget the pain. Do we need Ciampino?"

"Yes, please," said Tom as he pulled the passenger door shut only to have it bounce back open. Stretching out his arm, he once again took hold of the door's inside handle and pulled the door shut with more power. This only resulted in the door bouncing open with greater force.

"Let me," Isabelle said as she leant across him to tug at the handle. Tom was afraid that this would aggravate her injury but it was too late as she was already leaning across him. "There's a certain, how do you say, knack." With that, she pulled the door to a close. "Sorry, I didn't mean to squash you," she said as she slowly raised herself to a sitting position.

Tom found that he was holding his breath and it wasn't through fear for Isabelle but due to a sudden and acute awareness of her closeness. He now released the oxygen from his lungs and readjusted his sitting position. "It's very warm today," he mumbled as he struggled to engage his seatbelt into a locked position. "Cloudy but nice."

Isabelle turned the ignition and the Renault gradually coughed into life. "Don't open the window otherwise you can't close it again," she instructed him as she quickly checked the rear-view mirror before rapidly pulling the car out into the Roman traffic. "Now, tell me, do you always accept lifts from strange women?"

"Whenever I can," he responded happily as he stared out through the vehicle's grubby windscreen. "This is very kind of you. Perhaps you would let me buy you some lunch by way of a thank you."

Despite the reason for his journey to Rome and the strange events that had occurred since his arrival, Tom was actually beginning to enjoy his adventure and why shouldn't he? He had taken two weeks' vacation from work and that in itself was enough to raise his spirits. He was seeing Rome for the first time and was being chauffeured by a beautiful French girl. All in all, things could be much, much worse.

Isabelle looked thoughtful as she navigated their way through the city and towards the airport. "Lunch is never free, is it, Tom?" she said after some contemplation.

Her tone was sad, which took some of the shine off Tom's rising spirits, and the meaning behind her statement was in need of an explanation. Believing that the best way of getting a person to talk was to keep quiet, he waited silently for Isabelle to continue. He didn't have to wait too long.

For Isabelle, it was difficult to explain. She was embarrassed by her predicament, which made it necessary for her to attach herself to a complete stranger. However, it was not the first time she had been so reckless, for indeed, that was how she came to be in this mess in the first place.

A memory of childhood suddenly sprang to mind. She had been bullied at school but instead of telling her parents, she had pretended that she was too ill to attend school the following day. Her concerned mother had called the doctor, who soon discovered that there was nothing physically wrong with Isabelle. Her mother had been very embarrassed and extremely cross with Isabelle but when the truth came out, her mother's mood had softened. "Remember, Isabelle," she had told her daughter. "It is always best to be honest, even if you are embarrassed by the truth."

Making up her mind, Isabelle decided to break the silence. "You might have guessed that I was in the hospital because my boyfriend beat me up," she stated awkwardly. "I should say my ex-boyfriend."

If she expected a reaction from Tom, she was disappointed as there was nothing in his deportment to suggest he had even registered what she had just told him.

"To be honest with you," she continued, "I'm very frightened that if he finds me, he will kill me."

Tom sat and listened in silence as Isabelle's story unfolded. Isabelle mistakenly took this as indifference on his part but nevertheless continued. Having begun her side of the story, she was not sure that she could have stopped even if she had wanted to. It now seemed to her that by revealing what she had endured, she was in some way unburdening herself. In doing this, she was also managing to put some perspective on what had happened and was now happening to her.

"I cannot go to the police because he is a policeman of rank who is very well thought of by his colleagues. I have no one here in Rome and almost everything I have is in his apartment, including my passport. I have nowhere else to go and am too scared to return to the apartment in case he will find me. I have little money, no credit cards, no friends and I hurt very much!"

A tear fell from her eye and divided one side of her face with a delicate glistening channel. "So that's why I am helping you." She sniffed. "Because I don't have a single idea of what else I should be doing right now."

Isabelle ended the sentence with a sharp intake of breath like someone regaining the surface after spending several seconds below water. For a moment, Tom thought that she was about to break down and cry but with evident effort, she gathered herself from within and regained her composure.

Tom gave her a blank look. "I was thinking maybe a Chinese restaurant," he said. "I fancy some sweet and sour. Do you like Chinese?"

Isabelle glared at Tom and was about to ask whether he had taken any notice at all of what she had confessed to him but his eyes told her that he had heard and registered every detail. Her temper vanished as quickly as it had appeared. "Chinese would be very nice, thank you, Tom," she said with a warm but delicate smile.

Isabelle was beginning to like this Englishman, even if his sense of humour seemed a little odd at times. He appeared calm and fairly laidback, which she found an attractive quality, especially when compared to her recent life with Luca who had a tendency to overreact and exaggerate just about everything.

Although she hardly knew him, she felt safe with Tom, he was kind and he was trying his best to cheer her up. It was very soon, yes, but Isabelle sensed that she was at last reawakening and remembering who she really was. Having spent months building up a wall around her, Isabelle was surprised at how fast she was now able to pull it down.

Chapter 18

The Grand Hotel Beverly Hills

The two nuns shuffled excitedly along the red carpet leading to the reception desk of The Grand Hotel Beverly Hills. Any initial misgivings that they may have had when referred to a hotel with such a glitzy title soon vanished as the two luxury starved sisters took in the elegantly tasteful surroundings of the hotel lobby.

"Oh, Assumptia, would you just look at the marble floor, isn't it beautiful?" said Magdalene as her head flitted from side to side as if she were in a dream and trying to memorise every single detail before she awoke to find it gone.

"Aye, Maggie," Assumptia huffed happily at her side. "The Grand Hotel Beverly Hills and look there's the bar. I don't know about you but I have a whistle that's in serious need of a wet."

Once they had checked in and deposited their cases in their room, the two sisters sat together in the small but cosy bar and enjoyed a relaxing afternoon tipple. Assumptia's tipple consisted of an extremely large whisky, whilst Magdalene sipped elegantly at a small glass of amaretto.

They were almost alone amongst the dark wood and cushioned comfort of the bar, which was currently devoid of other guests. The barman seemed busily employed cleaning ashtrays that already appeared clean and making sure that the sisters had an adequate supply of peanuts and other assorted bar nibbles.

"So, Maggie, just run it by me one more time if you don't mind," Assumptia slurred as she lounged comfortably in the well-padded armchair. "Tomorrow you want us to go to the Vatican so as we can catch a glimpse of the Pope standing way up on high." Assumptia waved a large beefy hand nonchalantly in the air. "On his balcony. And by seeing the Pope standing there up on his balcony, you believe, for some reason only known to yourself that we can get God's forgiveness for us doing away with the old man."

Assumptia's blunt fingertips came down to rest with her other hand upon the well-filled tumbler contentedly balanced upon her substantial paunch. "And after that, we'll be fully absolved and OK to get on with the rest of our lives without fear of retribution and eternal damnation. Is that or is that not an accurate summing up of where we're currently at, Magdalene?"

"Well, Assumptia," Magdalene began primly. "I'm not quite sure that I would have put it quite like that myself but you do appear to have the gist of it." Sitting straight backed as always, Magdalene raised her small glass to her lips, which she no more than dampened with the rich aromatic liquid.

"And how are you going to get God's forgiveness?" Assumptia resumed. "I'm sorry to labour the point but I'm finding it difficult to understand because you say that you're going to say a prayer in the Basilica, at the altar under which it's said that St Peter himself is buried. OK, so you say your prayer and then what? What I'm asking, Maggie, is how will you know whether the Big Fellow forgives you or not?"

Assumptia shifted her position in the chair and took a large gulp of whisky. "After all, even though the old bastard deserved what he got, it's still a tall order to ask to be forgiven for doing him in."

"I hear what you're saying, Assumptia, and believe me I've given this a great deal of thought myself. The way I see it is that we have done a bad thing, a very bad thing and even allowing for the circumstances as they were, it doesn't detract from the fact that patricide is frowned upon."

"Amen to that," Assumptia interjected lazily. Choosing to ignore her sister's interruption Magdalene continued, "Tomorrow, when we pray in St Peter's, we must beg God to either forgive us or to give us some sign of his wrath. I pray that he will know how cruel Father was and that he will understand our actions and forgive us for our sin."

"So, what you're saying is that unless he strikes us down with a thunderbolt or some such, then we're in the clear," Assumptia said over a whiffy burp.

"That's about the size of it," Magdalene confirmed.

Assumptia pulled herself into a more upright position and this enabled her to reach across the small roundtable and give Magdalene a gentle pat on the hand. "In that case, I think we're home and dry but what'll we do if he himself sends a contrary sign?"

"Well," said Magdalene thoughtfully, "that would very much depend upon the sign. For example, if we were both to be struck down on the spot then we'd know that he's extremely cross with us. However, if the sun disappears behind a cloud and we get heavily rained upon, then we'd know that God is angry but content to forgive us provided that we take our punishment."

"Mmmmm," Assumptia mused. "What if the sign is somewhere in the middle of the two you just mentioned? What if he don't smite us down immediately like, but the sign he sends makes it pretty clear that he's totally pissed off with us?"

Magdalene once more moistened her lips with amaretto as she considered what they should do in the event that they remained alive but forever cursed. "I think in those particular circumstances that we should immediately return to Ireland and give ourselves up to the authorities."

"In that case," said Assumptia as she finished off her whiskey and slammed the empty tumbler down upon the table. "Just in case this is either my last day alive or my last day of freedom, I think I'll get pissed! Barman!" she called. "Same again if you don't mind but don't be so stingy with the measures this time."

Chapter 19

Setting the Trap

Luca thought it was strange that the telephone's ring should make the apartment sound empty but it did. The room was dark because the curtains were drawn and he sat quietly in the gloom holding a framed photograph of Isabelle in happier times. He tried to ignore the persistent ringing but eventually stirred himself to get out of the chair and answer the phone.

"Casaraghi," he announced gruffly into the receiver.

"Luca, this is Luigi Pesto."

"Yeah, what do you want?"

"I understand that you're looking for someone," Luigi cut straight to business.

"That's right I'm looking for Issi…Isabelle. Can you help?"

"I pay you to help me, Luca, not the other way around. I need something doing and I want it done quickly. But I'm a nice guy so if you agree to do this favour for me, then I'll give you some news about your girl."

Luca looked down at the photograph he still held in his hand and saw Isabelle smiling up at him through the gloom.

"What do you want?"

"I want you to find and kill Alfredo Caprietti."

This got Luca's full attention. "Don't be stupid. People have spent the last fifteen years looking for Alfredo Caprietti. What makes you think that I can find him now?"

Luigi didn't like being called stupid and made a mental note to teach Casaraghi a lesson that he'd never forget, just as soon as the bum had rubbed out Alfredo Caprietti. "Because Luca, I'm going to tell you where to look."

"I'm listening."

"His mother has been admitted to Regina Elena Hospital and Alfredo Caprietti was seen there with her earlier today. My guess is that he'll be back and when he is, I want you there to give him a special welcome home present."

"And where's Isabelle?"

Luigi began laughing cruelly. "Thanks for reminding me, Luca, I nearly forgot to tell you. She's shacked up with Alfredo Caprietti!"

"What!" Luca exclaimed in disbelief.

"Ask Franco, he saw the two of them together and looking real sweet too. She sure didn't waste time getting over you."

Luca slammed the phone down on Luigi's sneering laughter before turning to hurl the photograph against the wall with shattering ferocity. "You bitch! You dirty fucking slut bitch!" he screamed at the wall. "I'm going kill your new man! I'll cut out his fucking heart and force it down your filthy lying fucking French throat!"

He pulled open a drawer and withdrew an automatic pistol. Checking the clip, he shoved the gun into the belt of his jeans before buttoning his leather jacket over the top. Snatching up his car keys, he stormed out of the apartment and made his way toward Regina Elena Hospital and his revenge.

Chapter 20

Sleeping Partners

The car died when it reached the hotel. It had successfully carried Isabelle and Tom to the airport, where reclaiming his luggage had proved much easier than expected and ferried them back into the centre of Rome. Isabelle was in the process of guiding them into a vacant parking slot immediately in front of the hotel when the little Renault coughed abruptly before conking out completely.

Luckily the road sloped in the direction they were aiming, and the two passengers sat silently holding their breaths as the vehicle coasted the remaining few yards. When the car bumped against the kerb, Isabelle applied the hand brake and they both breathed out.

"It has never done that to me before." Isabelle sounded amazed at the vehicle's behaviour.

"Look on the bright side," said Tom as he gazed through the night towards the hotel entrance. "I don't think it's ever going to do that to you again. Don't forget to turn the lights off."

The car's headlights illuminated and magnified the drizzling rain, which was quietly but incessantly turning the city's streets into dark mirrors for the neon shop signs.

"That's the kind of remark I have already learnt to expect from you."

Choosing to ignore this remark, Tom got out of the car and pulled his holdall out after him. "I checked the hotel out on the web before I booked and it looks fine," he said as he made his way towards to hotel's revolving door but was halted as Isabelle called after him.

"Tom!" He looked back to see her standing forlornly beside her even more pitiful looking car. "Tom, I guess it is time now that we said goodbye."

He looked across the few yards that separated them. Isabelle had her arms folded about herself as she tried to keep out the evening chill. The darkness accentuated her pale complexion and he wasn't sure if the rain made it appear that she was crying or disguised her tears.

"Why?" he asked.

Isabelle didn't answer but neither did she walk away. Tom stepped closer. "What about if we come to an agreement?" he asked.

Isabelle gave him a questioning look.

"Why don't we stay together?" Tom continued, "Stay together until you want to go or I want you to go."

Isabelle continued to look at him questioningly.

"Look," Tom persevered. "I'm not suggesting anything even remotely biblical here so please don't think that I'm trying to seduce you." Tom was disappointed to note that Isabelle almost burst into laughter at this, but he continued resolutely. "I'll probably be here for at least a week or two. At the moment, you've nowhere to go and so you're welcome to stay with me until you sort yourself out."

In the face of her continued silence, Tom ran out of things to say. "Look Isabelle, I don't know what else to say."

"That's good," she responded. "I'm getting very wet standing here listening to you. Let's check-in and then we can think about eating something." She stepped forward took his arm and pulled herself close to him as if she was hoping that he would radiate some heat into her. "I suppose we are sharing a room, yes, in which case you might have to sleep in the bath."

"It's a risk I will have to take," he responded as they turned and walked into the Grand Hotel Beverly Hills.

*

Feeling extravagant, Tom had booked a double room for himself but now he had Isabelle to consider, he tried to change it to a twin room. Initially he had toyed with the idea of stretching his holiday budget to book Isabelle into her own room but the hotel was full with no further vacancies or room changes available. Therefore, a double room it was but upon arrival, he was relieved to find that what from the website he'd originally thought was an enormous double bed (and his reason for booking a double room) turned out to be two single beds pushed closely together.

"Look, Isabelle," he said smilingly as he lifted the bedspread to reveal where the two beds met. "No sleeping in the bathtub for me tonight."

Isabelle smiled wanly and dark circles under her eyes reminded Tom that his companion was far from well. "Hey, look, Isabelle," he said suddenly concerned. "Sit down before you fall down. I'll fix you a drink from the minibar and run you a hot bath. Are you due to take any more tablets?"

Tom pulled out a chair for her, which Isabelle ignored preferring instead to sink tiredly upon the bed. "I have no clean clothes," she slurred exhaustedly as she struggled to kick her boots off. "I suddenly feel very tired indeed."

Tom went to the minibar. "What would you like to drink?" he asked her.

"A brandy, please, Tom."

Tom heard the clump of a boot hitting the floor and so he knew that Isabelle's efforts had at least met with some success. When he turned around, he saw that she was now propped up against a pillow, her head lolling down against her chest. "Isabelle!" She jumped suddenly alert once more. "Try to stay awake for just a little bit longer. I'll run that bath I spoke of and also order something for us to eat from room service."

He had to wake her again when the bath was ready. He'd put some bubbles into and deposited the glass of brandy on the side of the bath. "I have no clean clothes," she mumbled feebly as she limped one boot on and one boot off into the bathroom.

"There's a robe in the bathroom, that'll have to do for a while," he answered. "Throw your clothes out and I'll get the hotel to launder them, you can look for some new ones tomorrow."

Her head appeared from behind the bathroom door, her eyebrows crossed in a look of concern. "I think not," she said brusquely. "Hand me the bag and I will put my clothes in there myself."

Tom smiled as he fetched a laundry bag from the wardrobe. Placing this in Isabelle's outstretched hand, he took up the room-service menu and began reading out what was on offer whilst Isabelle listened from the comfort of the hot bath. They both decided on steak and Tom phoned down the order and also arranged for the laundry service to collect Isabelle's clothes.

The laundry people were surprisingly quick at coming to collect the soiled garments and Tom felt bad about having to disturb Isabelle again. "Isabelle," he called from his side of the bathroom door. "The laundry people are here, I'm sorry but I need that bag." He could hear the fall of water as she raised herself from the bath and a small gasp of pain as she stepped out of the tub. Clasping a towel to her front, she opened the door to hand Tom the laundry bag. Tom's breath caught in his throat at the sight of her, she looked very beautiful and vulnerable in the soft pink testimony to her bath. As he took the bag from her hand, his eyes took in the steamy reflection in the mirror behind her, which remained distinct enough to show the ugly welts and bruises left by Luca's beating. He quickly cast his eyes downwards, took the bag and turned to deliver it to the lady who stood at the door ready to receive it.

*

Isabelle appeared very relaxed during dinner and Tom suspected that this had much to do with the painkillers she'd washed down with brandy. Dinner over and the food trolley reloaded and parked outside the room, they were both relaxed and enjoyed the bottle of Chianti he'd ordered with the meal. They now lay propped up upon their respective beds, Isabelle wrapped snugly in a white bath robe and Tom still fully dressed apart from his shoes. He'd moved the beds apart whilst she was still in the bath.

"This is nice, Tom," she slurred. "I feel *much* better."

"That's good, Isabelle," he answered, "I think you should get some sleep soon, you look like you need it."

"You say the nicest things," she giggled. "That's because you're nice. I like you, Tom!"

He just smiled. For some reason, Tom had always had a problem with drunken women, he thought that inebriation somehow cheapened them but with Isabelle it was different, she seemed to become softer and childlike.

"You're not like Luca, he was horrible!" she continued with a shudder. "I came to Rome with my boyfriend Pierre. I met Luca then, Pierre was not pleased and he went home all by himself…poor Pierre…if he hadn't seen that film Gladiator, maybe we would be married now."

Tom wondered why alcohol often made people want to confess and hoped that Isabelle would fall asleep before she said something that would terminally mar the mental picture he'd already painted of her.

As if sensing his discomfort and deciding to ignore it completely, Isabelle took another gulp of wine and continued her story. "He wasn't always horrible, you know. Once upon a time he was nice, too, just like you, but sexy."

"Thanks very much," Tom mumbled whilst staring at the ceiling as if something incredibly interesting were happening above their heads. Isabelle finally heard what she'd said and almost choked in mid swallow as she burst out laughing. Her laughter was infectious and any hurt that Tom may have felt at her remark was soon washed away.

Crying with hilarity whist complaining that it made her ribs hurt, Isabelle struggled to regain her composure and almost succeeded on several occasions before dissolving into laughter again. She looked gorgeous as she rolled from side to side on the bed wearing nothing but the white bathrobe. She clutched her ribs to protect them and although Tom had already seen her cry many times that day, these tears were heart-warming to behold.

Eventually she managed to regain control of herself and shakily getting to her feet, she leant over Tom (who remained perfectly still whilst looking up into her two watery blue eyes) and said, "you're very sexy too," before planting a soft kiss on the end of his nose. With that, Isabelle tumbled back on to her own bed and giggled some more.

A few moments later, Isabelle quietened down and rolled over to face Tom. "Tom?" she slurred seriously. "Why are you in Rome alone? Is there no Mrs Tom or special friend for you?"

"No, well least ways not anymore. I'm here by request." He went on to tell Isabelle about his father and the dying wish that Tom try to find the Italian girl he'd met during the war. He pulled out the bundle of envelopes from his holdall and they examined them together before setting them aside to look at the Madonna in the casket and the creased photograph of a young girl.

"This is very romantic," Isabelle said sleepily. "You would expect this more from the French and not so much from the English."

Tom just grunted at this for like all true Englishmen, he believed that there was nothing that a Frenchman could ever do that an Englishman could not do twice as well. Isabelle was barely awake and so he replaced his father's memorabilia in his holdall and set about turning the lights off.

He was just about to make his way to the bathroom when Isabelle's sleepy slurred voice drifted through the darkness. "Good night, Tom, thank you for being so kind."

"Good night, Isabelle," he replied. "I hope you feel much better in the morning."

"It's bizarre, you know," Isabelle slurred dreamily.

"What is?"

"The long-lost love of your father, Maria Caprietti."

Tom stood at the bathroom door and waited for a few seconds but when Isabelle failed to explain, he asked; "What's bizarre?"

But Isabelle had fallen into a deep exhausted and intoxicated sleep, and as Tom peered through the darkness towards her, he was greeted by a gently rumbling snore.

Chapter 21

Doctor Mido

Franco waited miserably across the street from the hospital. It was dark now and had been raining for the last hour and so he was wet as well as cold. His recently plastered arm rested in its sling within the confines of his leather jacket, and it hurt like hell. He couldn't remember the last time he'd had anything to eat or drink and he didn't know how long his Uncle Luigi expected him to keep watch on the hospital.

Whilst waiting, Franco had been thinking about his life and had just reached the sad conclusion that it was little more than one great amalgamation of bad days. His life was a book that no one would care to read, and upon which some stupid bugger had spilt his coffee leaving every page stained. What made things worse was that the previous twenty-four hours ranked amongst the worse he'd ever had.

He was trapped. Tonight, he was trapped in the rain outside a hospital, and tomorrow he'd be trapped somewhere else at the whim of his fat bullying uncle. If it was not for the constant pressure he was placed under to prove himself, he would not have got involved with Little Lui's hare-brained scheme of breaking into the Rialto Diamond Workshop. Nor would he have to contend with psychopathic policemen that broke bits of him just for the fun of it.

Had Franco not been born a Pesto, and had he not inherited what being a member of Rome's controlling criminal family entailed, then he would have liked to own a vineyard or write a book. Something rewarding and calm that would not involve him wasting his nights standing alone in rain and freezing his nuts off whilst hoping to catch a glimpse of an underworld celebrity.

He checked his mobile phone for the hundredth time that evening but there were still no messages or missed calls. He was hoping that Uncle Luigi would release him from his duty and send him somewhere warm and dry, or maybe even send a car so that Franco wouldn't have to stand in the rain.

Squeezing the phone in frustration, he shoved it back into his jacket pocket and turned his attention once more towards the hospital doors. Of course, this wasn't the only entrance, he mused not for the first time and wondered how his uncle expected him to keep watch on the whole frigging hospital. Alfredo Caprietti and Luca's French girlfriend could have come and gone a dozen times already without Franco being in a position to notice. This was stupid, really stupid. Franco made up his mind that he would phone his uncle and let him know his misgivings. Once more pulling the mobile phone from his pocket, Franco hit the number two speed dial and waited to be connected.

Franco heard the receiver being lifted at the other end and was greeted by Tony Lambretta's dull blunt voice. "Yeah."

"Hello, Tony, this is Franco. Is my uncle there?"

"Yeah."

It took a few seconds for Franco to register that as far as Tony was concerned, he would need to be a bit more specific. "Tony, would you please let my uncle know that I'd like to talk with him?"

"Yeah."

With that, Franco heard Tony replace the receiver and cut off the connection.

"Jesus fucking Christ!" Franco exclaimed angrily. "Why am I surrounded by people like this? I deserve more truly I do." He again pushed the number two speed dial button and was relieved to hear his uncle's voice answer at the other end.

"Hello, Franco, is that you?"

"Sure thing, uncle, I was jus—"

"Where are you phoning from?" Luigi interrupted.

"Outside the hospital…why?"

"Better make it a quick call so you can get back inside and watch Maria Caprietti like I told you to."

Franco cringed as the weight of own stupidity came crashing down on him. "Sure thing, uncle," he responded shakily. "I was just phoning to let you know that Alfredo hasn't returned yet."

"That's good, Franco, but you keep a close watch and let me know just as soon as you do see anything. How's Luca doing? I bet he's really pissed off."

"Luca?" Franco asked in confusion before quickly recovering. "Yeah he's pretty pissed off, uncle, that's for sure." Why Luca was pissed off and how Franco should know about it was beyond him and it was only instinct that had made him answer his uncle in the way he did.

He heard his uncle chuckling on the other end of the phone. "You're doing a good job, Franco, I'm almost proud of you. Now get back in that hospital and let me know if Caprietti shows his face again." With that, there was an abrupt click, and the line went dead again.

Holding the phone at arm's length and glaring at it as though it were the thing he despised most in all the world, Franco blew a long and angry raspberry before shoving the phone deep within his pocket and turning to make his sodden way towards the hospital.

*

The young woman at the hospital's reception desk looked up at the sound of Franco's squelching approach. He looked forlorn and dejected and reminded her of a puppy that she had had as a small girl. The puppy had been a mongrel and quite ugly really, but she had loved it very much.

There was something about this careworn little man that immediately appealed to her caring nature, and she greeted him with what she hoped was her warmest smile. "Hello sir, and how may I help you?"

Franco instinctively glanced over his shoulder to see who was standing behind him. People were not generally polite to him and he couldn't ever remember being smiled at by a pretty girl before. There was one occasion some years earlier when he'd had cause to take a bus and had found himself sitting opposite two pretty young girls. They had smiled in his direction and giggled lots, and this had made him feel handsome and desirable.

Then one of the girls had plucked up enough courage to speak to him and Franco had donned what he believed was his coolest persona before leaning forward to listen to what she had had to say. His ego had been immediately and rapidly deflated when he discovered that the only thing that had fascinated the young girls about him was the fact that the right shoulder of his jacket had been covered in greenfly.

Standing at the reception desk with his head cast shyly downwards, Franco could have been mistaken for someone who was trying to memorise his shoes.

Gulping audibly, he raised his head to meet the still-warm smile of the young receptionist. "I'm Maria Caprietti looking for," he mumbled disjointedly. "I she was this morning that she was admitted to your hospital this morning." Franco clenched his teeth and bunched his fists in frustration at his own idiocy before clearing his throat and starting again. "I'm sorry, I meant to say that I'm looking for Maria Caprietti and I understand that she was admitted here today." Franco always suffered a speech impediment when speaking to women.

The receptionist quickly tapped the details Franco had given her into her PC and gazed intently at the screen as she waited for a response. "Are you a family member?" she asked as she waited for the information to download. "Perhaps you could run your head under the hand drier in the restroom?"

"Yes and yes," Franco responded. "I'll do that before I visit Mrs Cap—my aunt. It's a great idea I wouldn't have thought of that myself."

"Oh," the receptionist beamed with pride. "I have lots of ideas. Would you like to hear about them sometime?" Her soft round face suddenly flushing red in shock at her own forwardness. "I finish in about twenty minutes and so we could grab a coffee or something once you've seen your…your aunt."

Franco could not believe what he was hearing. He had heard about this sort of thing happening to other people, albeit not often but it had certainly never happened to him before. "You're kidding me, right?" he asked suspiciously.

Now an even deeper shade of red, the receptionist fluttered her eyes nervously as she tried to ease the deep discomfort she now experienced as she braced herself for what she believed was to be imminent rejection. "I, I just thought that we, you and I might, it might be good if we went out for some coffee. It's OK if it's inconvenient for you," she said giving Franco an easy and painless way out if he chose to take it.

"No," said Franco dumbly. "No, that'll be great."

Franco was rewarded by such a huge beaming smile that he was left in no doubt as to the young woman's integrity although her motive remained a mystery.

"That's great!" she exclaimed. "I'll meet you back here just as soon as you've finished with your aunt. She's in room 26, second floor and the elevators are at the end of the corridor." She indicated to the direction of the elevators.

"Great." Franco smiled stupidly as he made to follow her directions.

"And don't forget the restroom," the receptionist added helpfully.

"Great," said Franco who continued to smile gormlessly. He held up a curly and wet length of his hair as proof of his intention to carry out her suggestion before turning and making his way towards the elevators.

Franco felt his heart sore within him as for the first time in his life he experienced true elation. *Perhaps today wasn't such a bad day after all*, he thought as he tapped the elevator's call button with his grubby index finger.

*

The first thing that Maria became aware of was the light, which slowly filtered through the various levels of her unconsciousness to find her spirit and guide it gently back to wakefulness. Next was the rhythmic and somehow comforting beep of the machine at her bedside.

Her eyes fluttered open and she took in her surroundings. She was lying on her back in an unfamiliar bed the linen of which was crisp and white. She had a tube in her arm that led up to a clear bag of liquid. She was also attached to the bleeping machine. She glanced at this machine and a moving green line confirmed that her heart was still beating strongly.

The room was small, brightly lit and tidy. In addition to the bed on which she lay, it had a television, a wardrobe, a chest of drawers, two chairs and some items of medical equipment.

Maria was extremely thirsty. Without moving too much, she managed to glance back over her head and as expected found the small hand unit from which she could summon assistance. She reached out with her free arm and easily managed to take hold of the unit. She was just about to press the large orange button when the door to her room opened, and a white coated doctor walked in.

He looked at Maria intently from behind a pair of horn-rimmed spectacles as he quickly closed the door and came over to her bedside. There was something about this man that was very familiar to Maria. He pulled up a chair and sat close to her, so close that she could read his name badge. He was Doctor Mido.

The Doctor took her hand in his and Maria thought that he intended to check her pulse but instead he lifted it to his lips and to her surprise he gently kissed it.

"Alfredo," Maria said shakily.

"Hello, Mama," said Alfredo Caprietti. Maria could see the tears spill freely from her son's eyes as he held her hand close to his face. "I thought I'd lost you, Mama. I thought I waited for too long."

"Alfredo," Maria whispered softly. "You should not be here, someone will see you and—"

"What will they see, Mama? I am fifteen years older and the years have not been kind. My hair is very thin and my face very fat. I am no longer the pretty boy that ran away. It's so good to see you again, Mama."

Alfredo stood so that he could embrace his mother and they both wept with happiness. "Ah, Alfredo," said Maria as her son released her and sat back down. "You're still very handsome just like your father." This reminded Maria of something. "Tell me, Alfredo; were you here at the hospital when I arrived?"

Alfredo looked thoughtful. "No, Mama, I only arrived in Rome today. I came back to wish you happy birthday. I wanted to be with you on your special day but you were taken ill. I only found out that you were at this hospital about three hours ago. Why do you ask?"

Maria thought for a while before dismissing the confused memory of her hospital arrival as a symptom of her illness. "No reason, Alfredo," she said as she looked lovingly upon her son. "Now why don't you tell everything that you've been doing all of these years? There must be lots to tell because you've been away a very long time."

"I will, Mama, I promise but I must go soon. Don't fret, I shall come back to see you many times but I cannot stay long, it's too big a risk for me. No more than ten minutes each visit. But as soon as you are out of here, I will take you away with me forever. Somewhere safe and then you can spend all day listening to my stories."

"That sounds wonderful," Maria said happily. "I will try to get better as soon as I can."

*

The elevator binged to announce its arrival on the second floor of the hospital and Franco stepped out. In a flash, two strong hands grabbed him by his jacket lapels and launched him violently back into the elevator's interior where he crashed noisily against its steel wall. The force of the impact was such that it knocked the wind from his body and Franco crumpled in a heap. Someone followed him into the elevator and pushed the button that sent them in the direction of the hospital's underground car park. He then stooped and reasserted his grip on Franco's lapels before heaving him to his feet and again banging him roughly against the steel interior of the elevator.

"Going down, Franco," Luca demanded maliciously through gritted teeth. Franco didn't have enough air in his body to respond verbally and instead nodded his head negatively. "I wasn't asking you, Franco, I was predicting your future!" With that, Luca brought his knee up sharply to smash into Franco's unprotected groin. Franco doubled up in agony, his face quickly flushing with colour before draining to a deathly yellowish grey. Luca again pulled him straight and again slammed him against the steel wall of the elevator. "I hear you have some news for me, Franco. So, if you value your miserable little life, you better tell me what you know and quick."

Franco gazed dazedly at Luca. His breath was coming in short pain and terror filled gasps as he fought to control his body enough to enable him to respond to Luca before he decided to inflict more pain upon him. "I saw her today...Isabelle. She was here...at the hospital...and she was with Alfredo Caprietti."

The elevator binged and its doors opened to reveal the dimly lit subterranean car park beyond. "What was she doing with Caprietti?" Luca demanded angrily.

"I don't know, truly I don't," gasped Franco. "I just saw them together, that's all. He must have come here because his mother is here. She's in room 26 but I don't know why Isabelle was with him."

Luca continued to hold Franco in place whilst he decided whether or not to be satisfied with this explanation. After some seconds, Luca accepted Franco's version of events and launched him unceremoniously out of the elevator to send him sprawling on the tarmac of the car park. Without a word, Luca hit the number two button of the elevator leaving Franco alone sobbing in misery and pain.

*

The elevator returned to the second floor and Luca stepped out and made his way to room 26. The door to that room was closed but as he reached for the door handle, it suddenly swung open. Blocking his way was a tall, powerfully built man who was wearing the white coat of a doctor. There was something about this man, an aura that immediately intimidated Luca and made him take an instinctive backwards step.

"My name's Doctor Mido," said the man as he removed his horn-rimmed spectacles and placed them in his breast pocket. "What is it you require from Mrs Caprietti?"

Momentarily lost for words, Luca starred at the imposing presence of the doctor. Luca guessed the man must be close to sixty years of age but he'd obviously taken incredibly good care of himself as Luca could detect a hard muscular frame beneath the white coat. Recovering himself, Luca pulled out his police identity card for Doctor Mido to inspect but in doing so, his wallet slipped from his hand to fall at Doctor Mido's feet. Doctor Mido bent easily to retrieve the wallet and after inspecting Luca's warrant card, he flipped the wallet shut and handed it back to the policeman.

"And how may I help you, officer?" Doctor Mido inquired politely.

"I need to ask Mrs Caprietti a few questions," he said.

"Why?" the doctor asked bluntly.

Luca cleared his throat. "That's between me and Mrs Caprietti."

The doctor's eyes bored into Luca. They were black like the eyes of a shark and Luca was not a man easily intimidated being more used to being the dominant force in any one-on-one situation. However, he now felt far from comfortable.

"I'm afraid that that is out of the question," said Doctor Mido. "Mrs Caprietti is in no condition to answer any questions at the moment. Now if you don't mind, I must ask you to leave and allow my patient to rest."

Doctor Mido guided Luca back towards the elevator and waited with him until it arrived to take the police officer away in the direction of the ground floor.

Alfredo Caprietti may have been away from Rome for more than fifteen years but nonetheless he remained well informed about who was who back in his hometown. Therefore, he was well-aware whose pocket Officer Luca Casaraghi was in.

He would need to keep a closer eye on his mother and those interested in her than he had at first believed.

*

Franco was in the restroom trying his best to tidy himself up, which was a difficult exercise because of his plastered and slung arm. He was in a great deal of pain and would ask the young receptionist for some tablets. His gaunt and shabby reflection stared back at him from the restroom mirror and Franco despised what he saw. Yelling in frustration, he launched a kick at a waste bin and sent its contents spilling out across the floor. Whimpering in pain and misery, Franco lowered himself painfully on to all fours before setting off to tidy away the used paper hand towels that now littered the floor. His back hurt too much for him to stoop. Once he'd completed his task, he slowly and awkwardly raised himself into a standing position, took another glance at his dejected reflection and made his way out of the restroom and towards the reception desk.

The girl was waiting for him. She was quite small and attractively plump, and she gave Franco a beautiful warm welcoming smile. She had removed her uniform and now wore jeans and white pumps, and a long brown leather coat over a red turtleneck sweater. Her thick dark hair fell in waves that nestled around her shoulders and to Franco, she was the most beautiful thing he'd ever seen.

"Hello," he said shyly as he approached. "I guess it's time I should tell you my name. It's Franco." Franco held out his hand, which the receptionist took with a small nervous laugh.

"Franco Caprietti, right?" she asked as they shook hands.

"No, it's Franco Pesto," said Franco. "Just like the sauce."

"Well, I'm very pleased to meet you, Franco Pesto. My name is Sarah Macaroni."

"Hey, that's funny," said Franco. "Macaroni and Pesto, we were made for each other."

Sarah continued to smile at Franco as she took his good arm and led him out of the hospital. "I do hope so, Franco," she said warmly as they stepped out into the night.

Luca was standing by the hospital entrance smoking a cigarette. He looked up as Franco and Sarah passed. "Well, well, well," he said sneeringly. "It looks like dog boy has found himself a girl."

Franco wanted to pick up the pace and keep on walking but Sarah pulled him to a halt and turned them both to face Luca like a cat ready to protect her kittens. "Are you talking to us, mister?" she asked aggressively.

Luca smiled evilly at the pair. "No, fatso," he replied. "I was talking to that worthless piece of shit that's dangling from your arm."

Sarah made to fly at their persecutor but Franco held her back. "Come on, Sarah, let's go, he's not worth it." At first, she was unwilling to comply but after a few moments, she allowed herself to be pulled back by Franco who urged her to hurry her pace so that they could get as far away from Luca as possible.

They had just crossed the road when Luca called after them. "Hey Franco, looks like your girl has bigger balls than you, or maybe she just walks that way!"

Franco could feel Sarah tense at his side but he kept a firm hold on her as he guided her further away from the hospital.

"Who is that vile pig?" she asked angrily.

"Would you believe he's a police officer?" Franco responded.

Sarah stopped dead in her tracks. "He's a what?" she demanded. "I will report him to the authorities; he cannot go around behaving like that."

"Forget it, Sarah, please," Franco begged. "Let's not let that bum spoil our evening. I want to hear about all of your good ideas. I don't want to talk about people like him."

Franco nodded towards where Luca remained standing and smoking his cigarette. As he did so, his uncle's limousine pulled up outside the hospital and as he watched he could see Tony Lambretta get out and open the door for Luigi Pesto.

"Who are those people, Franco?" Sarah asked as she watched the two men approach the rude man at the hospital entrance.

"I don't know," Franco responded absently as he watched and saw Luca nod in his direction. Luigi Pesto and Tony Lambretta both turned to stare across the street towards Franco and Sarah.

Luigi Pesto pulled the large cigar from his mouth. "Franco! Where the fuck you going?" he bellowed.

Franco turned to Sarah and felt his heart fall to his knees. "Maybe some other time?" he suggested lamely. Sarah looked back at him in bewilderment. "I'll make it up to you, Sarah, I promise I will but that's my uncle and he needs me."

Sarah just stared at Franco in open-mouthed disbelief.

"Franco, you useless shit!" Luigi roared. "Get your sorry arse over here right now otherwise I'll break every bone in your frigging body!"

"Like I said, he needs me," Franco continued miserably. "I'll be in touch real soon, Sarah." With that, he leant forward and pecked her on the cheek before turning and making his way back towards the people he loathed most in the whole world.

Chapter 22

The Divine Message

Sunday morning dawned bright and clear, with not a single clue to evidence the previous night's rainfall. Tom lay awake in bed staring at a patterned dance of dappled sunlight and cedar leaf which moved across the room's high ceiling. The open window and slightly pulled-back curtain not only allowed filtered sunlight but also the early morning murmurs and scents of Rome.

It had been a disturbing night in which he'd been dragged awake by Isabelle's struggles to escape her nightmare infested sleep. Her cries and shouts in the dead of night had been unnerving but he'd done his best to comfort her and rock her back to peacefulness.

Now, as he glanced across at her sleeping calmly in the adjacent bed, he wondered again at what possessed some people to be so callously cruel to others. He also wondered how Isabelle had ever managed to get herself mixed up with someone that could treat her so viciously.

She needed to get out of Italy as soon as possible. He would discuss this with her when she awoke and they could decide whether it was worth risking a visit to Luca's apartment to retrieve her passport or whether they should simply go to the French Embassy. Whatever was decided, he wanted to help in any way that he could.

His thoughts were interrupted by the S.O.S. signal that beeped out from his mobile phone to inform him that a text message had arrived. Without this spur, he might have lain in bed longer but as he was only a very infrequent recipient of text messages, he was intrigued to learn who was writing to him early on a Sunday morning.

Having retrieved his mobile phone from the top of the television set, Tom took it into the bathroom so that he could switch on the light and get a clearer view of the message.

HELLO THOMAS RICHARD HARRISON AKA TOM DICK AND HARRY. BET YOU DON'T REMEMBER ME? HERE'S A CLUE, THE GOOD SAMARITAN?? I STILL HAVE YOUR DAD'S LOVE LETTER. WHEN ARE YOU COMING BACK TO GET IT? LOVE ZOE X

Tom smiled at the message and the memory of the cheeky vampire look alike that had sent it. He decided to respond and quickly thumbed out a reply.

WILL COME AND CU WHEN BACK IN UK. STILL LOOKING FOR LONG LOST LOVE. PLAN TO SEE POPE TODAY. HOPING 4 DIVINE INSPIRATION. WHY U UP SO EARLY?

Having sent the message, Tom decided to take a shower and get ready for the day ahead. Whilst in the shower, he thought about Isabelle asleep in the room next door and was disturbed by a sudden and unexpected pang of guilt. For some reason, his brief and innocent communication with Zoe nipped at his conscience and the more he tried to dismiss the feeling as nonsense, the more severe it became.

Climbing out of the shower, he grabbed his phone and deleted Zoe's message and his reply. No sooner had he done this then his phone beeped out the S.O.S. signal to notify him that another message had been received. The sudden beeping had startled Tom and he'd almost dropped his phone into the lavatory but had somehow managed to catch it again before it hit the bowl.

GOOD TO HEAR THAT YOU'RE STILL ALIVE. CAN'T WAIT 2CU AND HEAR ALL ABOUT YOUR ADVENTURE. TAKE CARE. LOVE ZOE XX PS. NOT UP EARLY, UP REALLY LATE. JUST GOT HOME XX

Tom groaned inwardly and immediately deleted the message without responding.

*

He'd managed to get washed and dressed without disturbing Isabelle but when he returned from breakfast to find her still asleep, he wasn't quite sure whether or not he should be overly concerned. He set down her laundered clothing, which upon his return, he'd found hanging outside the door, and also the croissants and jam he'd brought for her from the dining room. Crouching down beside her, he shook her gently and was rewarded by a grumbled whine as she turned away from him and buried her head under the covers. "From that, I'll take it that you're OK and simply require some more sleep," he said happily relieved that Isabelle appeared to be suffering from nothing more threatening than fatigue.

Checking his watch, he discovered that it was now almost 10:00 and if he were to find the Vatican and witness the Pope's public address, then he had just two hours in which to do so. He quickly found a pen and paper and wrote Isabelle a note telling her that he was off to see the Pope and also leaving his mobile phone number, should she wish to contact him. He also left some money because he knew that she had none.

Satisfied that he'd taken care of everything he could, he grabbed the small, folded map of Rome, given to them at check-in, and excitedly took off in search of the Vatican.

His plan was simple. He would make for the River Tiber and once he reached that he would turn left and follow its flow until he reached the Ponte Sant'Angelo. From the map, it appeared that by crossing the river at this point, he would find himself at the beginning of the Via della Conciliazione. This seemed to be a long and perfectly straight road that led from the far side of the bridge right into the heart of St Peter's Square.

Leaving the hotel and turning left, Tom soon found himself in a pleasant park. He hadn't realised that the hotel was so close to the Villa Borghese, which he planned to visit at some stage during his stay. It really was a glorious day and the fresh spring had Tom feeling enlivened and full of reawakened zest. It was as if his spirit had been released from long captivity and allowed to soar freely in the warm air currents above the ancient beauty of its surroundings.

He almost laughed out loud when he heard Dean Martin's voice crooning "Amore" from the direction of a hot dog van.

Then a new noise made him turn and he saw a classically decorated hot-air balloon raise its human cargo high above the park. He decided that he would return there later with Isabelle and together they would go up in the balloon and see the sights of Rome from above. Also, the balloon made a good reference point should he become lost on his travels. He guessed that he should be able to see it from practically anywhere in the city just so long as it was airborne.

By chance, he came across what appeared to be the entrance to an underground railway station but on closer inspection proved to be a subterranean walkway complete with shops. Deciding to take a chance, Tom followed what pedestrian traffic there was and was delighted to find that the tunnel eventually expelled him close to the Spanish Steps and much closer to his destination than he had thought.

As Tom continued his journey he became aware of two things. Firstly, the general condition of motor vehicles was poor with many cars and vans displaying evidence of a collision at some time or another. This might be explained by the standard of parking, which was truly appalling. On several occasions, Tom had come across examples of double and even triple parking.

The second and even more disturbing thing was the degree of dog mess that littered the pavements. At least Tom presumed that the multitude of obnoxious brown piles he was forced to circumvent was the product of the canine population of Rome. *No wonder the ancients built aqueducts*, he thought glumly whilst sidestepping yet another fetid obstacle.

Despite this unpleasant distraction, Tom was nonetheless enjoying himself and checking the map and his watch, was pleased to note that he was making good time. Taking a succession of small side streets, he eventually made it to the river and had only to cross a large and busy road to make it to the embankment. Looking up, he saw a crossing about a hundred yards up from where he was standing and so set off in that direction. As he approached the crossing, he noticed that it was, in fact, a crossroads, the right junction of which was one of the bridges spanning the Tiber. The traffic lights appeared to be out of action as the police were busy directing the traffic.

According to his calculations, he shouldn't be that close to any bridge and so, as he walked he opened the map out in front of him so that he could reassess his position. It was then that it happened. As soon as he felt his foot sink into the soft yielding mass he guessed the worst, which was immediately confirmed by a resultant odorous stench.

"Shit!" exclaimed Tom as he hopped his way out of the danger zone. "This whole city is paved with shit!" He hopped a few jumps over to a stone plinth, which conveniently was of a shape that would allow him to scrape some of the muck from his shoe. Grimacing in disgust, he set about trying to rid himself of as much of the noxious substance as he could.

A shout made him look up to see a uniformed and sun glassed policewoman making her way towards him. As she approached, she let rip a fusillade of angry Italian lingo. Tom stopped what he was doing and it was only then that he noticed that the convenient plinth was, in fact, the base of an ancient statue of one of the city's forefathers.

"Sorry," apologised Tom doing his best to look contrite. "I didn't see—"

Hands on hips the policewoman stuck out her chin towards Tom and snarled at him in extremely good English. "Do you also deface monuments in your own country or is this a privilege you have saved for Rome?"

Lost for anything else to say, Tom tried apologising again but could clearly see that it was having no effect upon the irate officer. Fortunately for Tom, fate intervened and the blast of a hooter immediately followed by a screech of brakes and a sickening crunch suddenly provided the officer with a task more important than ticking off an itinerant tourist. Tom was not slow in seizing his opportunity and quickly left the crime scene.

To his surprise, the bridge turned out to be the Ponte Sant'Angelo and so he made his way across and was soon confronted by yet another set of traffic lights. These lights were working and as he waited for the little red man to be replaced by the green walker, he gazed up the long broad avenue that is Via della Conciliazione, to see the magnificent cupola of St Peter's Basilica resplendent in the spring sunshine.

He was filled with devout emotion and for a second, he believed he had an appreciation of how pilgrims to this most holy of places must feel when seeing St Peter's for the first time.

Tom would have enjoyed dwelling on this thought for a little longer but was disturbed by the excited chatter of two nuns who had arrived to stand beside him at the crossing.

"Well, there it is now, Magdalene, and have you ever cast eyes on anything so beautiful in your entire life?"

"Oh, Assumptia, it's beautiful, I wouldn't believe how lovely it is if I wasn't right here seeing it with my own eyes. Praise the Lord!"

For some reason Tom reached up and felt the golf ball sized bump on the top of his head. There was something about these two that was setting off all kinds of alarm bells within him but for the life of him, he couldn't guess why.

The lights changed and the green walker appeared and so Tom commenced his journey up the avenue towards St Peter's Square and the Vatican City.

*

Assumptia wasn't good on her feet and didn't enjoy walking. As she'd reminded Magdalene several times that morning, she was a martyr to her bunions. Therefore, progress had been slow and Magdalene had whimpered and fretted that they might miss the Pope's address unless Assumptia could push her pain to one side for the morning and not insist on stopping at every café they passed along the way.

As it turned out the sisters arrived in St Peter's Square at 11:15 and had a full forty-five minutes to spare before the Pope was due to appear on his balcony high above the assembled throng of tourists and homage payers.

"Well, Maggie," Assumptia puffed. "We might as well pop in to the Basilica now to say our prayers. At least then we'll be able to enjoy the Pope's chat in the sure and certain knowledge that God has forgiven us for all of our wrongdoings."

Magdalene looked at her sister thoughtfully and just when Assumptia thought her suggestion was about to be rejected, Magdalene gave her a bright smile and nodded her assent.

"Assumptia, you're absolutely right," said Magdalene. "Let's go ahead and do what we must to receive redemption for our sins. Then we can go about and enjoy the rest of our lives without fear and free of guilt."

Assumptia raised an eyebrow at her sister. "Maggie, are you not even the slightest bit worried that God might not be as forgiving as you expect? I mean we did murder our father and all."

"On a day like today, Assumptia," Magdalene beamed brightly. "I think the Holy Father would forgive us just about anything!"

*

Tom stepped expectantly into the cavernous, spiritually daunting interior of St Peter's Basilica and was not disappointed. The immense devout grandeur of the building was staggering to behold.

Although not overly religious, Tom could not help but be impressed. The air inside hung dark, and heavy with time, like a low-lying cloud of piety, the aura of which impelled visitors to instinctively bow their heads and reflect upon their own insignificance in the face of God and all his mighty works.

Gazing up into the deep, time laden gloom, he was quickly captivated by the shafts of bright sunlight that arrowed through the living darkness from small windows cut high into the massive walls. These bright darts exposed mighty painted images of God and heaven and brought to life swirling dust eddies that danced sombrely around ancient saintly images.

Not for the first time he wished he had someone special to share these sights and feelings with. He again thought about Isabelle asleep in the hotel room, but he didn't allow his thoughts to wander too far down that particular road. He couldn't deny that he liked her and hoped that something would develop between them but he wouldn't be in the least bit surprised if it didn't.

The Basilica was making him reflective, too, but he didn't think God would approve of some of the thoughts that quickly passed through his mind. Pushing all such feelings to one side, Tom made his way across the marble tiled floor towards the Altar.

There were quite a few sightseers within the Basilica, mostly Japanese tourists but the size of the place made Tom doubt that it could ever become truly crowded.

When he reached the Altar, Tom stood with one foot upon the topmost marble step and dwelt on the implausible thought that St Peter, the Apostle of Christ was buried beneath his very feet. The bones of a man who had actually broken bread with the son of God rested no more than a few feet from where he now stood.

It was then that Tom's nose was reminded of the previous incident with the dog's mess. He drew back in horror, aghast to see that his shoe had left a disgusting brown smear upon the Altar step. He felt his face burn in embarrassment and shame as he continued to step backwards unsure of what he should do. He decided to get out and turned to flee from the Basilica, all the while hoping that no one had seen what he'd been responsible for.

As he quickly made his way towards the exit, he noticed the two nuns that he'd seen earlier at the crossing and they seemed to be making their way towards the Altar. For some reason, Tom stopped, his eyes following their tracks with morbid fascination as his hand subconsciously lifted to the bump on the top of his head. Something inside him told him exactly what was about to happen and he could have prevented it by rushing to stop the nuns but for some reason he was rooted where he stood and powerless to stop what had been ordained.

Reaching the Altar, the two Sisters fell awkwardly to their knees in supplication and kissed the marble step.

Time stopped. Tom remained where he stood; holding his breath as well as his bump as he waited for the inevitable. Even the Japanese tourists seemed to sense something momentous was happening as their chattering and camera clicking began to fade and die.

As one the nuns raised their heads from the step and turned to look at each other. From where he stood, Tom could clearly see the look of shock and disgust displayed upon the faces of the poor women. It broke the spell he'd been placed under since seeing the nuns within the Basilica and he quickly turned away and made good his escape.

"Well, Magdalene," Assumptia spat bitterly as she roughly wiped the fetid stain from her mouth with the sleeve of her cardigan. "Did you get your message?"

Chapter 23

Late Arrival

When Isabelle finally awoke she was famished. She checked her watch and it read 12:00. Groggily wondering how she had managed to waste an entire morning asleep in bed, she kicked her way out of the bedcovers and climbed shakily to her feet.

The surrounding silence told her she was alone but the plate of jam and croissants reassured her that she had not been entirely forgotten. As Isabelle tucked greedily into her late breakfast, she noticed the note and money left by Tom. The note was short and matter of fact but reading it, Isabelle felt sad that she was not with him. She hardly knew him but she felt safe in his presence, and cared for. Absently, Isabelle gazed at her dishevelled reflection in the bedroom's large ornate mirror as she considered these feelings. Finding no answer in her sleep puffed eyes, she sighed in resignation of her failure to understand herself and instead helped herself to another croissant.

Stretching carefully, she waited for signs of pain and when these arrived, they were not sharp reminders of injury but fainter duller memories. Nonetheless, as a precaution, Isabelle took some more painkillers before making her way to the bathroom to prepare another bath.

A few minutes later, she was nestling comfortably amongst mountains of white bubbles. The hot soapy water felt good against her skin and as she relaxed her mind drifted lazily back to Tom's story. He was here in Rome trying to find the long-lost love of his dead father so that he could deliver to her the love letters his father had written more than sixty years earlier. A beautiful tragic story that was full of sadness. How could Tom ever hope to find this woman after all this time? Was it possible that Maria Caprietti was still alive and living here in Rome? If so, she must be very old and…

With a start, Isabelle sat up straight in the bath and the violence of her movement causing soapy water to spill over the tubs rim and splash noisily on the floor below. Climbing quickly from the tub, she made her way into the main room and grabbed the telephone receiver. She stood there naked and dripping as she waited for the hotel's reception to answer.

The old woman who had grabbed Tom at the hospital, Isabelle was sure she had heard one of the medical staff refer to her by the same name as the woman Tom was searching for. The old woman had called Tom Alfredo! Tom's father's name was Aflie, Alfie, Alfredo! Isabelle was convinced that by some strange quirk of fate Tom had unknowingly found his father's lost love before he'd even begun his search in earnest.

"Hello, yes, this is room 317. Would you please connect me with the Regina Elena Hospital? Yes, everything is fine, thank you."

As she waited impatiently for the connection to be made, she hoped Tom would not decide to choose that moment to return to the room and find her naked and dripping wet. She leant forward and grabbed a sheet from her bed, which she clumsily wrapped around herself whilst still holding the telephone receiver pressed against her ear.

"Hello, yes, I wonder if you could help me," Isabelle said as soon as she was connected to the hospital. "I'm phoning regarding Maria Caprietti, she was admitted to your hospital yesterday. Is she still…yes…I'm her daughter. She is much improved, good and visiting times? Room 26, yes that's very helpful, thank you very much. Goodbye."

Isabelle was both stunned and elated. Could it really be the same woman? Almost in a daze, she replaced the receiver. Suddenly snapping back to life, she reached for the paper on which Tom had left his mobile phone number. Reclaiming the telephone, Isabelle dialled Tom's number and waited for his answer. When it came, it was obvious to Isabelle that Tom was walking at quite a pace as his voice was punctuated by heavy breaths.

"Hello, Tom. It's me, Issi."

"Hello, Isabelle, sorry, Issi. How are you feeling today?"

"I'm fine, Tom. Now, listen."

There was something in Isabelle's tone that immediately got his attention. Tom was walking along the Vatican side embankment of the Tiber. He'd chosen an alternative route for his journey back to the hotel, which led him beneath the shady trees that lined each bank of the ancient river. Spotting a convenient bench, Tom sat to listen to what Isabelle was intent on conveying.

"What is the name of the Italian woman you are searching for?"

Isabelle was talking quickly and Tom could detect the excitement in her words. "Maria Caprietti. Why?"

"Tom, I think I've found her!"

Tom was shocked but before he could ask any of the numerous questions that popped into his head, Isabelle continued her story. "That old woman who grabbed you in the hospital, it was her. She is Maria Caprietti. I phoned the hospital to check and that's her name. She's staying there in room 26."

Tom was silent as he took in all that Isabelle was telling him. After a few seconds, he was able to respond. "OK, Issi, I'm on my way back to the hotel now. I'll get a cab if I see one but it should take me about an hour at most to get there."

"No, Tom, you're closer to the hospital than to the hotel. I will meet you there."

Once Isabelle had explained to Tom how to get to the hospital, he was pretty sure that he'd be able to find it without too much difficulty.

"Issi, the letters and the other stuff, they're in a blue carrier bag within my holdall. Would you please bring them with you?"

"No problem."

"And Issi."

"Yes."

"Thanks."

The line went dead and Isabelle was left holding the receiver to her ear and staring again into her own eyes reflected by the ornate bedroom mirror. She felt overjoyed at helping Tom and excited about being involved in his adventure. She also suddenly felt incredibly sad, and as she stared into her own eyes, she saw tears begin to gather.

"No, it's not happening," she told her mirror image. "It's too soon and you do not even know him."

With that, she unravelled the bedsheet and set about getting dressed.

*

Luca gave Franco a sideways look. It was now Sunday afternoon and they'd both been keeping watch at the hospital for almost twenty-four hours. Luca was beginning to feel like Franco looked. *Give it another month or two without sleeping or washing*, he thought, *and we'll be like twin brothers.*

They hadn't spoken much because Luca had no interest in anything Franco had to say and Franco was too scared to say anything to Luca.

For Luca, there had been just one highlight throughout their vigil, and that was when Sarah, the fat receptionist, had shown up for work. For a short while, Franco had been as happy as a pig in shit. He'd suddenly sprung into life and skipped over to greet her, all smiles and pleading. She had left him for dead, not even taking the trouble to acknowledge his existence. That had made Luca laugh so much he'd almost choked and the more miserable Franco had become, the more Luca laughed. *What a worthless piece of shit*, Luca thought not for the first time.

Luca and Franco now sat side by side in the hospital's reception area and despite receiving a few curious glances from the security personnel, they had not been troubled. It wouldn't matter if they had for Luca would have just waved his police warrant card under their noses and that would have been the end of it.

"I need a coffee," said Luca who felt he needed lots of things but decided to opt for something obtainable. Franco didn't respond and this irked Luca. "Shithead," he said nudging Franco spitefully in the ribs, "I said I need a coffee."

Still ignoring Luca, Franco changed seats for the empty one next to him. "If I have to tell you one more time, Franco, I swear I'll break your other fucking arm," Luca growled menacingly.

Franco was about to retaliate when he saw that Sarah had just swapped places with a colleague and appeared to be making her way in the direction of the hospital cafeteria for her lunch. "Fine, I'll get you a coffee," he said as he stood and left Luca sitting in the hospital reception.

Hurrying to catch Sarah, Franco's large feet slapped noisily upon the polished green tiles of the long corridor. "Sarah!" he called plaintively at her back. "Please wait." At first, Sarah ignored his pleas but when his calls became embarrassingly loud, she stopped and waited for him to catch up.

"Hi Sarah," Franco said shyly as he approached the waiting receptionist. "How are you doing today?"

Sighing in exasperation, Sarah turned and continued her journey. After a second's hesitation, Franco shuffled along next to her. "I guess you're pretty annoyed with me?" he asked as they approached the swing doors leading to the cafeteria.

Sarah stopped and turned to face Franco who flinched in the face of her withering glare. "Franco, why are you here?" she demanded. "This is a hospital, it's for sick people. Are you sick, Franco?"

"Well, no," Franco began. "I'm here…"

"To visit your aunt?" Sarah interrupted. "Who are you trying to kid? Don't bother lying to me, Franco, you're no more related to Maria Caprietti than I am. So tell me, Franco." Sarah jabbed a menacing finger in Franco's direction. "What are you doing here?"

Franco didn't know how to answer. He was at the hospital keeping watch on a sick old lady in the hope that her notorious son would pay her a visit. This would enable either his uncle or a mad policeman or both, to murder the old lady's son as well as the son's girlfriend. What was he doing here?

"What am I doing here," said Franco sadly. "Sarah, I only wish I knew how to answer that question."

"Well, only you can," said Sarah.

Franco looked into Sarah's honest round face and saw in it the simplicity and purity of one untarnished by life's darker side. She instinctively knew the difference between good and evil and would utterly embrace goodness and just as unequivocally reject evil in any of its many forms.

"I don't know, Sarah," said Franco with newfound resolve, "but I've decided to leave now and I will not be back…not unless I get sick or break something else," he said lifting his slung arm in emphasis. "I'm sorry for everything, Sarah, really I am. Take care."

With that, Franco turned and walked away. If he hoped Sarah would call after him, he was disappointed. But, she did watch him go and it did take a considerable effort for her not to call after him.

*

Luca stood when he saw Franco stride into the hospital reception area and make for the exit. "Hey, dog boy," he challenged as he made to block Franco's escape but Franco sidestepped him and continued towards the automatic doors with Luca in immediate pursuit. The doors sprung open and Franco stepped outside just as Luca reached out and grabbed him by the shoulder.

"Don't you dare ever turn your back on me," Luca raged as he pulled Franco around to face him. Franco did not resist against the force of Luca's pull but instead, tucking his chin into his chest, he used his head as a ram against the bridge of Luca's aquiline nose. The blow took Luca by complete surprise and he tumbled dazedly to the floor with blood gushing from his crushed nose.

Franco leant down and gazed into the dilated pupils of Luca's bewildered eyes. "Personally, I think it's an improvement," said Franco calmly. "Some people would pay thousands to have a hooked beak like yours altered, and you got it done for free." Then reaching out with his good hand Franco took hold of Luca's arm and helped him to his feet. "Come on, Officer Casaraghi." He clumsily brushed Luca down. "You'd best get cleaned up."

With that, Franco guided the stunned Luca back into the hospital and towards the washrooms. "It's lucky that we're so close to hospital," said Franco. "You might want one of the doctors to take a look at you." Still guided by Franco, Luca had a hand cupped under his nose to catch the blood that continued to gush from his wound. Sarah's replacement on reception pulled a sickly face as the two men moved past her towards the washrooms and decided to summon assistance. It was an extremely quiet day at the hospital and so a nurse immediately appeared to take charge of Luca.

Franco stood and watched Luca get escorted away by the nurse and they had almost disappeared from sight when he raised his arm and called, "Bye Luca, get better soon." He wasn't sure if Luca had heard him and didn't care. All Franco wanted to do now was to return home, have a hot bath and change his clothes. Then, for the first time, he would start to live his life the way he wanted to live it. He was his own person and not his fat uncle's pawn. So smiling wearily, he turned and again made his way to the exit and home.

*

Isabelle was feeling and looking much better. She would have preferred not to wear the same clothes two days running but at least they were clean. Before leaving the hotel, she had checked her reflection in the tall mirror on the inside of the wardrobe door. She considered casually chic a good description as she took in her black designer jeans and pointed boots of the same colour. Luca had once told her that she had a body built for sin but she quickly disregarded this unwanted memory because Luca had once said many things and most of them were lies. A tight white blouse accentuated her slim body and full breasts and the jeans and boots made her long slim legs look even longer and slimmer. "Poor Tom," she said to her reflection, "you don't stand a chance." She then pulled on the huge black coat that Luca had given her before taking another look in the mirror. "Then again, maybe you do."

*

Later as Isabelle entered the Regina Elena, her pain-filled visit of little more than twenty-four hours earlier seemed a distant memory. It was funny to think that all things considered she was happier now then she had been for some considerable time. Whilst she could hardly recommend the experience, her suffering at the hands of Luca had been a lifechanging experience which made her appreciate the normal everyday things so much more then she had done previously. Turning to not so normal everyday things, where was Tom?

Isabelle decided to check whether Tom had already made his way up to room 26 and so set off in the direction of the elevators. However, she stopped before reaching them and decided to wait for Tom at the hospital's main entrance. Isabelle thought it unlikely that Tom would not wait for her if he'd arrived first.

Luca made his way back to the hospital's reception area. His broken nose was swollen and stuffed with cotton wool which made it difficult for him to breath. The bruising had given him two black eyes and so he now resembled a panda with a sore muzzle. Worst of all was his vision, which kept losing its focus. He hadn't mentioned this to the medical staff for fear they would retain him at the hospital for further tests and observation.

He still found it difficult to comprehend that he'd allowed an idiot like Franco Pesto to inflict such damage upon him. Luca decided that his punishment of Isabelle would have to wait. He had a new priority and that was to kill Franco Pesto before the idiot blabbed his mouth off and destroyed Luca's reputation forever.

Luca gazed ahead of him and the world once again blurred and faded. Squeezing his eyes shut and opening them again, his vision cleared to reveal…Isabelle? She had her back turned to him and was slowly making her way out of the hospital. He was almost certain it was her…yes, he was sure, it was the cheating bitch! His luck was changing. Quickly devising a plan, Luca decided he would apprehend Isabelle, use handcuffs if necessary. He would wave his warrant card at anyone who tried to interfere and they would assume he was arresting a criminal and leave him to get on with it. He would drag her to his car and would drive somewhere remote and make her beg. If she begged real nice, he might let her live…for a little while longer at least.

He felt a stirring in his loins as he pictured the scene and set off in eager pursuit of his victim but pulled up short when his vision blurred again. *No,* he thought, *I'll take her to Franco's apartment and that should get everything sorted out in one go*. He squeezed his eyes shut again and opened them but the blurring remained. I'll make it look like he killed her then in remorse took his own life. As suddenly as it arrived the blurring cleared. "Here I come, ready or not," he said evilly to himself as he again set off in pursuit of Isabelle.

*

Tom was lost. He looked around him and could not see a single street sign to help him pinpoint his position on the map. Isabelle had made the directions sound so simple and now he didn't have a clue where he was. He again looked at the steady stream of traffic that poured down the busy road where he stood and hoped to see a taxi. He'd already seen several but none had stopped when he'd waved to them. Tom looked at his wristwatch. *Isabelle was bound to be at the hospital by now*, he thought.

*

Unaware of her peril, Isabelle meandered slowly towards the double doors. She was humming quietly to herself as though she hadn't a care in the world. *The benefits of a good night's sleep were truly amazing*, she thought lazily. A good night and an even better morning's sleep, she corrected herself as the automatic doors opened and she stepped outside.

Homing in for the kill, Luca was just about to follow Isabelle outside when his route was suddenly blocked.

"Well, if it isn't the charming police officer," Sarah sneered angrily. Intent on his victim, Luca made to push passed her but Sarah's stocky low-centred body made her a formidable barrier and she moved to block Luca's escape. "What's with your face?" she asked. "Someone take exception to being treated like dirt?"

Luca had no time for this. "Look, fatso, if you know what's good for you, you'll just get out of my way," he whispered angrily. Then gesturing towards his bruised and bloodied face, he said; "And you tell your ugly weasel boyfriend that he'll pay for this."

"You mean Franco did that?" Sarah said in amazement as she allowed Luca to jostle her out of his path. "I didn't think he had it in him." Sarah didn't bother to disguise the admiration in her voice.

Luca turned savagely and glared at the receptionist. "Mark my words," he growled. "Very soon, the dog boy will wish he'd never been born." With that, Luca stormed through the automatic doors.

Isabelle was still there. She hadn't moved and she was still looking away from him. He quickly made a grab for her.

Chapter 24

A Family Resemblance

Raising an arm, Isabelle waved. "Tom!" she cried out happily. "What took you so long?"

Luca grabbed nothing but air as Isabelle skipped lightly down the steps towards a man who had just crossed the road and was making his way towards her. Luca quickly ducked back inside the hospital, all thoughts of revenge on Franco temporarily forgotten.

"Blimey, Isabelle, you heal fast," said Tom cheerfully as he strode to meet her. "Are you feeling as good as you look?"

This made her giggle in delight. "That's lovely, Tom, I'm sure I'll make a Frenchman of you yet."

"There's no need to threaten me with horrible things," Tom rebuked. "I was only inquiring into your welfare."

They both laughed and Isabelle took Tom's arm and guided him towards the hospital. "Are you excited about meeting your father's ex-lover Tom?" she asked as they entered the hospital.

"I don't know what I am," replied Tom honestly. "I never spent as much time with my father as I should have and I regret that. There was always something else to do which seemed more important at the time. I think I took him for granted, I just thought that he'd always be around just waiting for when I was ready to spend more time with him. Now he's gone I miss him. I don't know, Issi, I just think that meeting this woman will make me feel closer to my dad for a short while."

Isabelle squeezed his arm caringly. "I hope so, Tom," she said as they stopped and waited for the elevator to arrive.

As Luca watched them, he was overcome by intense jealousy. His emotions raged within him and the physical effort it took to resist an impulse to gun them both down where they stood made him shake uncontrollably. Luca was in danger of spiralling out of control and as he watched his woman cosy up to the gangster Caprietti, he struggled to keep his fury in check. *Kill them, Luca, kill them both but not here and not now,* he told himself. *But soon, very soon, I'll listen to you both screaming.*

He knew they would be making their way to room 26 and so when Tom and Isabelle disappeared inside the elevator Luca made his way to the stairwell and followed them up. His breathing was laboured due to the damage to his nose and by the time he reached the second floor, Luca was panting like an old man and he tasted blood in the back of his throat. He carefully opened the stairwell door and peered cautiously along the corridor. Isabelle and Alfredo Caprietti were indeed standing outside the room occupied by Caprietti's mother. They seemed hesitant about entering. Finally, the man Luca believed to be Alfredo Caprietti reached up and knocked on the door.

Tom wasn't sure if he should wait to be beckoned into the room or whether he should just step in and introduce himself. "Open the door, Tom," Isabelle urged quietly. However, the decision was taken away from him as the door was pulled open from within by a powerfully built man in a white hospital coat. Tom looked at the man's face and took an involuntary step backwards. He was looking into the face of his father.

The man considered Tom and Isabelle slowly. *"Che cos'è questo?"* he asked in a stern voice.

Isabelle cleared her throat. "He wants to know what we want," she translated to Tom. Mistaking his obvious distress as nervousness at the prospect of meeting his dead father's wartime sweetheart, she impatiently tried to nudge him into action.

"English?" the man asked.

"I'm sorry," stammered Tom who was still trying to get over the shock of being confronted by his father's doppelganger. "We would like to see Maria Caprietti if that is at all possible."

"I am Doctor Mido," said the man in smooth accented English. Alfredo was about to turn Tom and Isabelle away with an excuse but there was something intriguing about the young couple. When he looked into the face of the man, it was almost as if he were looking into a mirror twenty or so years earlier. "I'm sure that Miss Caprietti will be delighted to see you," he said standing back to allow them clear access to the room.

Isabelle went first and Tom saw her nod and smile, blushing with embarrassment. As Tom followed her Doctor Mido announced to his patient in English. "Miss Caprietti, it seems that you have visitors from England."

Tom looked at Maria who was sitting up straight in her bed. She was old but Tom could see she was a proud woman. Her night dress was winceyette which reached right up to her neck. Her face was thin but remained smooth and her white shoulder-length hair was neatly brushed back. Her most startling feature was her eyes which were clear, dark and piercing. She stared intently at Tom.

As Maria looked at the young man, the mists of time cleared and she again looked at the English soldier she had loved so many years before. Never releasing him from her eyes, she asked Tom. "What is your name?" Tom was about to answer but Maria interrupted him. "It is Harrison, is it not?"

Doctor Mido dropped the clip chart he'd being studying, which fell to the floor with a clump. He turned to stare at Tom. Isabelle was becoming increasingly uncomfortable and sidled closer to Tom, whose eyes remained fixed with Maria's. "Tom Harrison," said Doctor Mido slowly. "I believe you knew my father."

Maria released Tom and looked towards her son. "I am a little tired at the moment, Doctor Mido, perhaps you would be good enough to show these people out."

Tom turned quickly to Isabelle and guessing his desire, she handed him the blue carrier bag containing his father's letters and other mementos. "Could I just give you these?" he asked as he approached the bed. "They're letters form my father to you. There's also a few other bits that you'll understand better than I."

Maria's eyes showed some confusion as Tom handed her the bag. "All the letters he wrote to you were returned unopened," Tom explained. "He told me a little about you just before he died and asked that I try and find you."

"Please, you should go now," interrupted Doctor Mido. Tom glanced at the doctor who also seemed strained as he ushered them towards the door. "Miss Caprietti is not well, she needs to rest. Thank you, if you don't mind."

Tom really hadn't known what to expect but being dismissed like an unwanted salesman came as a bit of surprise both to him and to Isabelle. As soon as they were out of the room, the doctor closed the door behind them leaving Tom and Isabelle thoroughly confused.

Isabelle was quicker to recover. "Come on, Tom, let's get out of here," she said as she took his hand and led him back towards the elevator. "This is too bizarre and anyway you have kept your promise to your father and that is the main thing."

Tom was too deep in thought to respond but he allowed Isabelle to lead him away. Something important had just happened and somehow he'd managed to miss it.

Chapter 25

Passport

By the time they stepped out of the hospital, Tom's confusion and disappointment had turned to anger. "She might at least have taken a look at one of the letters," he fumed at Isabelle. "Or asked what my father had told me about her or how he'd died or something, anything! Not even a bloody thank you."

"Now, come on, Tom, let's think about it," soothed Isabelle. "The last time she saw your father was during the war when Maria Caprietti would have been little more than a child. She might not even remember your father."

"Of course, she remembers him," Tom retorted angrily. They'd stopped at the top of the stairs leading down from the hospital's main entrance. "She remembers him so well that she could even see that I'm his son."

"OK," said Isabelle nodding thoughtfully as she accepted Tom's point. "Then they're two other possibilities that spring to my mind."

"Go on then," urged Tom who found himself doubting that Isabelle would come up with anything plausible.

"Well, first of all, it could have been Maria who returned all of your father's letters unopened. Therefore, when you show up sixty years later on your…pilgrimage for your father, she is less than happy to see you."

This was indeed plausible. It didn't make good listening so far as Tom was concerned but it did make sense. "And your other possibility," he asked as they turned and made their way slowly down the stairs. Isabelle took hold of Tom's arm as though it were the most natural of actions. He didn't complain, in fact he liked the intimacy of the gesture very much.

"The second possibility is that someone purposely kept your father's letters from Maria. So, the man she loves goes off to fight the Germans and she hears no more of him. She must think that he is either killed or pleased to be away from her. I don't know but let's just say that she thinks he is dead. Then many years later, her dead lover's young son shows up and everything…is changed."

Isabelle's words fell like a weight on Tom's heart. He cursed himself for not thinking things through before charging in on the poor lady and delivering a bombshell circa 1944.

"How could I have been so thoughtless?" he said, his words lined with self-loathing. "Jesus, I couldn't have made a worse cock-up of it if I'd tried."

Isabelle tugged him to a halt at the foot of the stairs and as he turned to face her, she cupped his face in her two slim long fingered hands and tiptoed up to kiss him long and gently on the lips. Tom was momentarily frozen but he quickly thawed and took her in his arms. Their mouths moved slowly and deliciously together until the kiss ended and Isabelle moved her face away and smiled sweetly up at Tom.

"Tom, I don't know why your father sent you on this…how you say?"

"Fool's errand," volunteered Tom.

"That will do. I don't know why he sent you but I'm pleased he did. And you have done nothing wrong. It's a miracle you ever found the woman but you did that in little more than twenty-four hours so you should be proud."

"Thanks, Issi." Tom smiled at the girl in his arms and as he looked into her eyes, he could not understand the depth of feeling he had for this woman he'd met only the day before. "I couldn't have done it without the sexiest French detective in the whole world."

Breaking the embrace, they ambled along happily together. "What shall we do now?" Isabelle asked after a while. It was as if she had been reading Tom's thoughts. "There is no need for you to stay in Rome and you cannot possibly leave me behind now that you have made me fall in love with you."

Tom doubted that she was serious about the love bit but recalling her earlier experiences, he was keen to get her away from Rome and Luca Casaraghi.

He delved into his jacket pocket and pulled out his mobile phone, which he handed to Isabelle. "Give Luca a call at home," he said.

Isabelle looked startled. "Why?" she asked nervously.

"To see whether he is there," Tom responded.

"And if he is?" she asked with incredulity.

"Hang up," said Tom matter-of-factly. "And if he isn't, we'll go and reclaim your passport."

"No, Tom, I cannot do it," said Isabelle in horror. "It is too risky, he will kill me if he catches me and he will probably kill you too."

"Listen, Isabelle," said Tom. "We'll phone now and if he doesn't answer, we'll go to his apartment. We'll phone again when we get there and if he still doesn't answer, we'll quickly get in grab your passport and get out. If we're lucky, we could spend tonight in England, France, Spain, wherever; and you'll be safe."

"And what if we're not lucky?" Isabelle asked desperately. "You do not know him, Tom, he is a mad man!"

"Look," said Tom taking Isabelle by the shoulders. "I promise that I'll not let anything bad happen to you, I promise. Now, do you trust me?"

Tears spilled from Isabelle's eyes as she nodded her assent before raising the telephone and calling Luca.

There was no answer because Luca was not at home. Luca was on the opposite side of the street sitting in his car and watching them intently.

Chapter 26

Love Letters

"Mama." Alfredo sat on the bed and gently rocked Maria back and forth in his arms. He hated to see his mother upset and in his advanced years deeply regretted being the cause of much of his mother's anxieties. This time it was different, the news brought by the young Englishman had affected her deeply and Alfredo held her close as great wracking sobs shock her old body.

"The letters," Maria sobbed. "There're so many letters from your father."

"I know, Mama," Alfredo soothed. "He must have loved you very much." Loosening his embrace, Alfredo gently dabbed away Maria's tears with his handkerchief. "I don't understand why you never received them."

Maria sniffed looked at her son through tear washed eyes. She sniffed and cleared her throat. "It must have been your grandfather's doing," she said breathlessly. "Your father never knew I was pregnant when the army left but I told your grandfather." As she spoke, Maria's eyes became unfocused, looking not at her son and the hospital's small room but back in time to when she was a young woman. "He took the news badly and that was only natural. He spoke of the shame that I'd brought upon him and the family. I told him that I was in love and that Alfredo…Alfie would come back for me as soon as he could. But your grandfather thought I was crazy to fall in love with a soldier, especially an English soldier. So, he sent me to stay with my aunt in Florence and that's where I stayed until after you were born. I didn't rush back to Rome even after that. There was nothing to rush back for, just memories. When I first went to Florence, I would call my father every day and ask him whether there was any news of Alfredo, your father, but he always said there was none."

Upon the bed scattered across its covers and sinking into the dip created by Alfredo's weight were tens of unopened envelopes. Each envelope had Maria's name and address scratched through and her father's neat writing instructing that they be returned to the sender.

"My poor Alfie," Maria said sadly. "He must have thought I didn't love him. If only he knew, if only he knew." Gasping suddenly, Maria became alert. "Alfredo, the boy!" she exclaimed. "Go after him quickly."

"Why, Mama, what's wrong?" asked a startled Alfredo.

"If you don't find him, he will be lost forever and there's so much I need to know that only he can tell me."

"OK, Mama," said Alfredo as he quickly got to his feet and took off the doctor's white coat. Folding it quickly, he opened the room's small wardrobe and threw it unceremoniously inside before making for the door.

"Alfredo!" Maria called.

"Yes, Mama," Alfredo answered turning his head back around the door he had just left.

"Bring your brother back to me."

The look on Alfredo's face showed no emotion. He simply nodded and made off in pursuit of Tom and Isabelle.

Maria gathered the letters together and slowly began to place them in date order. Once she had done this, she spent several minutes staring at Alfie's faded writing upon the first envelope before carefully prising it open.

My Dearest Darling Maria,

I hate being away from you. If I could, I would move heaven and earth to hold you in my arms tonight…

Chapter 27

Murder

"Tony!" Luigi Pesto struggled to pull his bulk out of the armchair. "Tony!" he called again his voice rising above the telephone's shrill ring. Mumbling to himself about things getting done quicker if he did them himself, he made his way to the telephone and lifted the receiver.

"Luigi Pesto," he announced in his dull monotone voice.

"You don't sound too happy, Uncle."

Luigi moved the receiver from his ear and looked at it as if expecting that it would give him some clue as to why his idiot nephew was sounding so pleased with himself. The Bakelite receiver provided no insight so Luigi returned it to his ear.

"Listen, Unc," Franco's chirpy voice piped into the earpiece. "What would you say if I were to tell you that I was leaving?"

Luigi winced at the casual way in which Franco addressed him. He also suspected that Franco's apparent jollity was insincere. Putting the two together, Luigi's instincts prepared him for trouble. "Goodbye?" he ventured vaguely.

"Hey, good one, Unc, you kill me, you really do."

"That's a distinct possibility Franco, now stop your clowning around and just tell me what it is you want!" Luigi's voice brooked no further nonsense. The line went quiet for a few seconds but Luigi guessed that Franco was just plucking up enough courage to get to the reason for his call.

"Uncle," Franco said at last. His voice had become shaky with emotion as he approached the crux of the matter. "I want to tell you." There was another pause.

"I wish you would!" Luigi interjected impatiently.

His uncle's angry voice was the spur that Franco needed. "I've had enough of you and of your kind of people. I hate you and everything you represent, and I just wanted to tell you."

At that moment, Tony Lambretta entered the room. He looked relaxed and smart in a striped open-necked shirt and grey trousers. The large half-eaten sandwich held in his right mitt tarnished the image somewhat but all in all, Luigi was pleased with the way his understudy was developing.

"Boss, your wife says…"

He stopped midsentence when he saw Luigi waving him to silence. Covering the receiver with his hand, Luigi beckoned Tony closer. "Hey, Tony, you should listen to this. It's classic. I'm taking Franco's confession."

Luigi aimed a large porky finger at the telephone's speaker button whilst simultaneously motioning Tony into silence.

Clearing his throat theatrically, Luigi leant close to the telephone. "It's good to talk, Franco, and I'm glad you took the time to share your feelings with me. Now, would you like me to share my feelings with you?" Stepping away from the telephone, Luigi beamed at Tony, he was pleased with his wit and enjoying this unforeseen opportunity to pour more misery and scorn upon his repugnant nephew. He was, however, taken aback by Franco's response, and the smile fell from his fat face.

"What did you say?" Luigi demanded into the telephone's voice box.

"I said I have no interest in the feelings of a fat egotist with the intellect of a slug," Franco repeated. "I think you're a prize shit, Luigi Pesto, you respect no one and are too stupid to realise that no one respects you."

Luigi looked at Tony in disbelief. "Can you believe that, Tony?" he asked. "He's gone crazy, he's lost his fucking mind!"

"So Tony is there, too," continued Franco. "Have you ever taken a close look at that crucifix he wears?"

Luigi looked at the crucifix hanging around Tony's neck. "Show me that," he said gesturing with his hand for Tony to move forward.

"No, it's nothing special, Luigi, it's just a crucifix and chain the same as hundreds of others," Tony replied seemingly unwilling to give Luigi a closer inspection.

"Tony," said Luigi forcibly. "I said, show me the frigging crucifix!"

Sighing deeply, Tony stepped forward, pulled the crucifix from his shirt front and obediently dangled it in front of Luigi. Luigi took the heavy cross in his hand and yanked it towards him. Despite his size, Tony was forced to take another step forward by the force of Luigi's tug, the thick gold chain suddenly becoming an ornate leash. Turning the cross in his hands, Luigi inspected it closely.

"Where did you get this from, Tony?" Luigi asked suspiciously.

"I can't remember, boss, I got it many years ago."

"Uncle Luigi," Franco chimed. "Tony and Aunt Sophia have become very close friends. He gives her something and she gives him presents."

Franco didn't like lying but he wanted to hurt his uncle and gain some small revenge for all the insults and pain that Luigi had poured upon him over the years. He wanted to strike back and this was the only way he knew how. He'd noticed Tony's large and gaudy cross and chain on several occasions and he was all too aware of his uncle's simmering jealousy.

Luigi's cold black fathomless eyes bored into Tony Lambretta's. "Have you been fucking my wife?" he demanded menacingly, his emotions like a volcano about to erupt.

Tony's head was being forced lower by Luigi's grip on the chain. This was frustrating Tony who was doing his utmost to finish his sandwich but each time he made to bite a chunk, Luigi would yank the chain taking his mouth away from its intended target.

Glancing up at his employer Tony smiled patiently. "Don't be stupid, boss, why would I want to do that?"

Whether it was because he referred to Luigi Pesto as stupid, or whether Tony's response suggested that he'd have to be mad or blind to sleep with Luigi's wife, it was the wrong answer and it caused Luigi's threatened eruption to explode.

Yanking the chain down violently, Luigi caused Tony's head to slam brutally against the hardwood desk on which the telephone was perched. With his free hand, Luigi reached out and grabbed a heavy marble figurine of Hermes the messenger of the gods and raised it high above his head. Tony's heavy lidded eyes gazed cow-like up at the figurine his head held tight against the desk as Luigi continued to pull down on the thick gold chain. "Say goodbye, Tony," growled Luigi as he made to crash the figurine down against the side of Tony Lambretta's head.

The blow never came. Instead, Luigi's face took on a startled look and he let the figurine fall from his hand to thump heavily on the carpet. "Goodbye," said Tony as he twisted the stiletto deep into Luigi's abdomen. Luigi released the gold crucifix allowing Tony to climb to his feet. Tony removed the stiletto before reaching up to take a handful of Luigi's hair. Pulling his head back, Tony gently forced the knife through Luigi's fat chins and up into his brain.

"Hello, are you still there?" Franco's voice piped through the telephone's speaker. "What's going on?"

Tony let Luigi's heavy lifeless body fall to the floor. Carefully wiping the blade of his stiletto on the dead man's white silk shirt, Tony replaced the blade before using his mouth to delicately remove fragments of crushed sandwich from his other hand. Unfortunately, most of the sandwich was entwined in Luigi's grey curled hair and there was no way that Tony intended on retrieving that. Reaching for the telephone, Tony lifted the receiver, which automatically took it off voice box.

"Hey, Franco, how you doing?" Tony asked congenially.

"Tony, are you OK?" Franco asked nervously.

"I'm fine, thanks Franco," he responded sedately as he perched his bum on the desktop. "Why did you tell Luigi, me and his wife were doing things behind his back?"

"Listen, Tony," said Franco nervously. "I didn't say that you and Aunt Sophia did anything bad. Uncle Luigi must have misunderstood. Did he overreact? He always has been dead jealous so far as Aunt Sophia is concerned."

Tony looked down at Luigi's corpse, which slumped on the carpet at his feet and he nodded sagely. "Well, Franco, from here on in, he'll always be at least fifty percent of what you say he is."

Franco frowned when he heard this as he didn't understand Tony's comment. "Is everything OK with you two?" he asked.

"I had to kill your uncle, Franco," Tony announced without feeling. "He tried to brain me and so I killed him. Now you listen to me, Franco."

Franco listened in shock and trepidation.

"I hope you're not interested in all that vendetta crap because if you are, I'm going to have to come looking for you. The way I see things, you're not really cut out for this business and your uncle treated you like dirt anyhow. So, I might have done you a favour by taking him out of your life. But, I don't want to spend my life looking over my shoulder. Do you understand, Franco?"

This was an extremely long speech for Tony Lambretta and he had Franco's full attention.

"I fully understand you, Tony," blabbed Franco. "And I promise you faithfully that I have absolutely no desire to avenge my uncle, none whatsoever, absolutely not."

"OK," said Tony. "Now here's the deal. I'm going to tell everyone that I walked in and found Luigi dead. Rumour is that Alfredo Caprietti is back in town and so everyone will think that Caprietti wants his throne back and has started work to make that happen. You, Franco, you can do what you like just so long as you keep your mouth shut and stay out of your uncle's business matters. Are we agreed?"

"Sure thing, Tony," Franco agreed enthusiastically. "What are you going to do, Tony?"

"Me," said Tony smiling. "I would like to get involved in the restaurant business. Maybe your Aunt Sophia would like the help. She seems to like having me around and I like helping her."

Franco didn't know what to make of this and so he simply wished Tony good luck and hung up the phone. He looked around the living room of his apartment, the décor of which would impress any visitor. Tastefully minimalist with calico walls and bleached wood floors. A chic mushroom leather suite with matching drapes and modern sharp-edged furniture. It was a far cry from the image Franco projected to the outside world. This was the real Franco the way he felt on the inside.

His outside appearance reflected the self-loathing he'd developed as a consequence of being trapped under the yoke of his uncle's expectations. And now, this yoke had been suddenly and unexpectedly removed. Franco searched within for some signs of emotion, and he found the first timid waves of excitement beginning to simmer deep in his belly before suddenly erupting like a geyser to fill his whole being with elation. Leaping up, he punched the air like a footballer who'd just scored the winning goal in a cup final. He felt like he'd just been released from a long-term prison sentence and he wanted to celebrate and he knew exactly who he wanted to celebrate with.

Chapter 28

Vampire

"I'll tell you what we are, shall I, Assumptia?" Magdalene sobbed noisily over a large glass of Chianti.

The two waiters who stood at the door of the small bistro and watched the nuns slumped together in the sunlight were bemused by the sisters' distress and would occasionally offer up to each other a possible cause for consideration. Outside the bistro and sat at a small round table that had a red and white checked cloth, Assumptia and Magdalene were close to finishing their second bottle of wine. But no matter how much they drank, the fetid taste of God's rejection would not be washed from their lips.

Assumptia looked up at Magdalene through two heavy bloodshot eyes as she waited for her sister to confirm yet again that their plea to God for forgiveness had been utterly rejected.

"We're damned!" Magdalene continued. "Utterly totally and without question or fear of contradiction, we are damned. D. A. M. N. E. D. Damned! Just one blemish, that's all it took. A lifetime devoted to the Lord, a whole bloody lifetime and just one little teeny-weeny murder and that's it, game over, you're out, finished, washed up, turned out and bloody well damned!"

Assumptia took a slurp of wine before replacing the glass a little too heavily upon the table. "It might be good if we got something to eat," she suggested slurring, "how about some pizza?"

"Pizza?" Magdalene repeated in disbelief. "Sister, we have just been denounced by God and you want pizza? Jesus, Mary and Joseph, can you credit it. We have nothing to look forward to but an eternity of hell and torment and the best you can suggest is a fucking pizza!"

Assumptia had never heard her sister blaspheme before and, as a result, was momentarily taken aback. However, she quickly gathered herself together and pulling up her sleeve she leant forward and dealt Magdalene a heavy slap across the cheek. This brought a startled scream from Magdalene and cries of consternation from the watching waiters. Assumptia's glare combined with a wordless Italian insult was enough to silence any further protests from the waiters.

"If our poor departed mother, God rest her soul, could hear you speak like that, she'd turn in her grave! Now would you ever get a grip of yourself, Magdalene, and stop making a show of us."

Sniffing deeply, Magdalene looked sadly towards her sister through tear dampened eyes.

"Oh, Assumptia, what is to become of us?" She sobbed piteously. "I just don't know what to do anymore."

Magdalene stretched out her hand and shakily lifted the large glass of wine to her lips. After taking a number of gulps, she put the glass down to reveal two small red trickles stemming from each end of her mouth.

Assumptia looked up and slowly pointed at Magdalene and began to laugh. "I know you say we're damned, Maggie." She chortled. "But there's no need to be impersonating a frigging vampire!"

A confused look crossed Magdalene's eyes as she tried to fathom the reason for her sister's mirth. Reaching into her handbag, she removed a small plain mirror and held it up so she might see what misfortune was so amusing her sister. First she saw her wine reddened and tear-stained eyes but by angling the mirror down, she was then confronted by a reflection of her reddened lip with matching dribble.

"Oh!" Magdalene exclaimed. Then attempting a Transylvanian accent, she said, "Would you look at that, ha bring me a burger and make it rare!"

Despite all that had befallen them and their bitter disappointment, the two sisters roared with laughter until the tears fell freely from their eyes.

"Do you know, Assumptia?" Magdalene chuckled. "I can't ever remember laughing like that. It feels so good, come to think of it, I feel good too."

"That's good," said Assumptia as she wiped moisture from her eyes. "I'm pleased for you, Maggie, truly I am and I'm pleased for me too."

"I know it's a wicked thing to say," Magdalene continued, "but for the first time in my life, I feel free."

Assumptia stopped what she was doing and looked intently at her sister.

Seeing the look on Assumptia's face Magdalene knew she had to explain herself further. "I'm free of Father and after today, I'm free of God, too. He doesn't want me anymore, you see. It's His choice and He chose not to want me. The truth is that I was getting mightily sick and tired of all that praying and grovelling anyway. So now that I come to think of it, being damned might not be so bad after all."

Assumptia had never understood what made her sister tick and Magdalene had never ceased to surprise her. However, this latest declaration filled Assumptia with misgivings.

"And what about me, Maggie?" she asked solemnly. "Would you like to be free of me, too?"

Magdalene smiled warmly at Assumptia and reached out a hand to cover one of Assumptia's meaty paws.

"Never, sister dearest," she said sincerely. "I would sooner lose my right arm."

Assumptia's face was brightened by a huge beaming grin. "That's good, Maggie," she declared brightly before changing the subject. "And where's next for two miserable sinners like us?"

"Why," Magdalene said without hesitation. "America, where else!"

Chapter 29
Surprises

Tom handed the taxi driver a 10 Euro note and waved away the proffered change. "Shall I ask him to wait?" Isabelle asked as Tom gazed up at the heavy façade of the apartment building where Isabelle and Luca had lived together. The otherwise bleak exterior was softened by tall windows with green painted wooden shutters and intricately wrought iron balconies some of which displayed colourful window boxes or large ceramic pots filled with flora.

"That sounds sensible," he said as he waited for Isabelle to climb from the car. Tom was already standing on the narrow and cracked sidewalk of the quiet cobbled street and was itching to get this dangerous errand over and done with as quickly as possible. His palms felt clammy and he had a hollow nervousness in the pit of his stomach. "Just hurry, please, Isabelle," he urged hoping that he sounded calmer than he felt. He told himself that it was only natural to be scared and that there was nothing to be ashamed of in feeling fear, it was how he handled his fear that was important.

Isabelle spoke in Italian to the taxi driver and climbed from the car. "He will wait," she said as she closed the vehicle's rear door to stand beside Tom and follow his gaze.

"They are much nicer on the inside," Isabelle said almost defensively, "the apartments are really quite big."

Tom gave her a sideways glance and raised an eyebrow. "It's OK, Issi, I'm not planning on moving in," he said as he handed her his mobile phone. "Now phone and see if lover boy is at home."

Isabelle flushed angrily at Tom's words and manner and she snatched the phone from his hand. "There is no need, Tom, no need at all," she admonished him as she keyed in the number with hard spiteful stabs of her finger.

"I like this even less than you do so please do not take your…your…shit out on me!" she raised the phone to her ear and when Tom tried to make eye contact with her, she turned her back on him and looked the other way.

Isabelle's anger irked Tom and he started to feel angry himself but his anger was directed at himself rather than at Isabelle. "That's long enough," he said to Isabelle's back, "let's go in, get your stuff and get out again."

Isabelle gave no sign that she had heard him but remained facing away with the phone still pressed to her ear. "Come on, Issi," Tom said and he reached out to her, "I'm sorry, it was a stupid thing to say. It's the nerves, that's all."

As he gently pulled Isabelle around, he was sad to see that she looked pale and drained. "I'm not sure that I can do this," she said as she looked up to meet his eyes. "I'm scared."

Tom wasn't now feeling quite so confident about the expedition himself. He had had the feeling for some time that he was being watched but he told himself that his nervousness was making him paranoid. Looking about him again, he saw no one. "Was there any answer?" he asked Isabelle and she shook her head negatively.

*

High above, Luca peered down at them through the long net curtains in the main room of his apartment. He smiled wolfishly as he witnessed their indecision. He had guessed that Isabelle would try to retrieve some more of her belongings and now he waited like a spider waited for its prey to stumble into its web. Pulling the pistol from his belt, he checked the clip before tucking the weapon into his trousers waistband at the small of his back. "Come on, Isabelle," he urged. "Come and introduce your new man to me." Luca was pleased with the way in which the situation had developed in his favour. He would gun down Alfredo Caprietti here in his apartment. He would then take a knife to Isabelle and when he had killed her, he would place the knife into the hand of the dead Caprietti. When the police arrived, Luca would be distraught as he told how when he had arrived home, he was confronted by Caprietti, a renowned felon, who had broken into his home. Acting in self-defence, Luca had shot and killed the knife wielding Caprietti only to discover that tragically he had been too late to save his poor defenceless and much-loved Isabelle. "*C'est tragique ma chère.*"

*

Tom took Isabelle by the hand and led her across the small, cobbled street to the entrance of the apartment. The entrance was blocked by a large and heavy green painted door which looked ancient but well kept. They expected to find the door locked but as Isabelle went to insert her key, the door swung silently open to reveal a large dark and cool hallway within. Tom glanced inside and was surprised and impressed at the hidden grandeur that lay behind the green door. A white marble staircase climbed silently upwards into the gloomy interior and this was edged by an ornately worked iron and brass banister. It filled Tom with a feeling of ancient permanence in which he felt small and alien. "Impressive," he mumbled as he entered the hallway and held the door open for Isabelle. She stepped nervously inside. "It's like something from Raiders of the Lost Ark," he continued as he looked about him. "What floor is the apartment on?"

Isabelle motioned for Tom to be quiet by placing a finger to his lips. He got the message and quietly closed the door deciding to leave it on the latch, just in case, they needed a quick getaway. With the daylight shut out, Tom was momentarily blinded and instinctively reached out for Isabelle. Isabelle's response to his touch was unexpected. At first, Tom was surprised as he felt her move into him and rapidly kiss his face, covering his eyes, cheeks and lips with soft warm kisses. His senses heightened by the darkness he could feel the softness of her skin and smell her delicate perfume as she continued to kiss him. Tom became suddenly aroused and pulled her tightly into him as he began to nip and kiss at her neck and chest. Isabelle moaned in pleasure as she pushed her groin into his legs.

"Make love to me, Tom," she gasped through their kisses. "Make love to me now."

For just one second, Tom thought of where they were and the dangerous situation that already existed, which for all kinds of reasons was about to be greatly exacerbated by their sudden passion. These concerns were extremely brief and soon washed away as Tom lost himself in the moment and began to tug at Isabelle's clothing to open up her bare flesh to his hungry touch. He released her breasts from the confines of her bra and kneaded the soft mounds before taking a large erect nipple into his mouth.

Isabelle fumbled with the belt of his jeans but was quickly able to release him from their restrictions. She kicked one leg out of her own trousers and gasped as Tom lifted her on to him. Their lovemaking was hard, desperate and all too brief but they climaxed together and were left clinging to each other and panting like they had just finished a marathon. They kissed again before pulling apart and quickly rearranging their clothing.

"I feel much better now," Isabelle breathed as she tucked her blouse into her trousers. To Tom, she sounded like someone who had just quenched a long thirst and he smiled at her through the cool darkness, which now seemed alleviated as his eyes grew accustomed to the dimness of their surroundings. "The apartment is on the second floor, are you ready?" He nodded and they set off hand in hand up the broad marble staircase.

*

Luca was becoming agitated, the journey from the street up to the apartment was taking them too long and he couldn't understand why. He had decided to conceal himself by standing in the bathtub with the shower curtain pulled across, this would allow him to pick his time to announce his presence and welcome the ill-fated couple to his humble abode. He had almost giggled with excitement and expectation when he had first entered the bath but now as he stood there holding his pistol ready he began to wonder whether his prey had had a change of heart and decided against such a risky and foolhardy venture.

The minutes passed slowly and Luca's strained efforts to detect any sound of their approach remained unrewarded. His patience finally failed him and he pulled back the shower curtain and stepped gingerly and silently from the bathtub. Carefully opening the bathroom door, Luca stepped stealthily into the hallway and made his way to the living room with the two large windows that overlooked the street. He peered down and could see that the taxi that had brought Isabelle and Alfredo Caprietti remained parked on the kerb below. Turning silently, he returned to the hallway and made his way towards the front door.

Reaching the door, he carefully made to place his eye against the spy hole situated in the centre of the door. It was then he noticed that he had absentmindedly engaged the security chain when entering the apartment. This discovery coincided with the sound of approaching footfalls. "Shit!" he cursed as he quickly attempted to disengage the security chain without giving himself away. He could hear the key being placed into the lock as he gingerly slid the chain out of position but there was no time to hide. The door swung open.

*

The door swung open to reveal a long hallway. It was bright and clean with a polished wood floor, a high ceiling and cream painted walls. "It looks nice," said Tom from where he stood in the doorway.

"Looks can be deceiving," responded Isabelle as she slid passed him and disappeared into the first door on the left.

"Shall I wait here?" asked Tom after a few moments as he was unsure about what he should do. His question was answered by the sound of the toilet flushing and then Isabelle reappeared.

"No, come in and close the door, Tom," she said as she made her way into the room directly opposite the toilet. Tom stepped inside the hallway and pushed the door closed behind him. If he had looked, he would have seen that closing the door had uncovered Luca's hiding place but Tom kept his eyes to the front and followed Isabelle.

Tom found Isabelle in a small bedroom which was evidently used for storage space. "This is the spare room," Isabelle announced with a smile. "It's where I keep...kept most of my things."

Tom looked around and saw a single bed, a chest of drawers and a wardrobe. There was also an exercise bike and a set of steel dumbbells arranged neatly on a triangular rack. "Those are Luca's," said Isabelle as she followed his gaze, "he likes to keep in shape."

"Bully for Luca," Tom said dryly as he took in the various bits and pieces that littered the room.

"You have nothing to be jealous of, believe me," Isabelle retorted.

Tom's planned protest was abandoned as he instead decided to accept Isabelle's offhand comment as a compliment to him as well as a slight on her former lover.

"Tom, would you please get that suitcase from the top of the wardrobe? It is mine and I need it."

Tom did as he was asked and lifted the old and battered case from where it lay on the wardrobe. Judging by the dust accumulated on its lid, it had lain there some considerable time. He handed the case to Isabelle and she busily set about opening drawers and cramming their contents into the case.

"Don't forget your passport," Tom reminded her.

As he watched her stuffing clothing into the case, Tom's foreboding suddenly and acutely returned, and he became anxious to be away from the apartment.

"Issi, please, the taxi is still waiting and this is risky. Let's just get your passport and leave."

Isabelle stopped what she was doing and turned to Tom. She no longer showed any fear or concern and instead her face was flushed with anger. "No, Tom, I'll not leave everything that is mine! I'll not do it, it's not fair! Why should I run like a thief in the night? I did nothing wrong, it was…"

"What was it, Isabelle?"

Tom jumped with fright and spun around to be confronted by a dark-haired man who was pointing a gun directly at him. The man looked far from well, he was bedraggled and unshaven, had two black eyes and a nose that had clearly only recently been broken.

"Luca," Isabelle's voice trembled. "Please Luca, no."

Luca sneered at her in disgust. "Prego, prego," he whined in Isabelle's direction. Tom remained silent although he had instinctively raised his hands in the air in a gesture of surrender. Turning his attention to Tom, Luca raised the gun to point it between Tom's eyes. The weapon was less than a foot away from Tom's face and there was no chance of evading the bullet.

"Ciao…Caprietti," Luca smirked.

Isabelle screamed and Luca pulled the trigger.

*

Alfredo Caprietti had seen Tom and Isabelle disappear in a taxi. Alerted by the sound of cars screeching to a halt and the angry blast of hooters, he had also seen a car driven by Luca Casaraghi pull dangerously out into oncoming traffic and set off in pursuit of the taxi. Alfredo knew instinctively that Tom and Isabelle were in trouble although he could not guess what possible interest they would be to Luca Casaraghi. Alfredo had managed to hail a cab almost immediately and had instructed the driver to follow the vehicle that held Tom and Isabelle. Although Alfredo's driver had initially managed to keep in touch with the

144

leading taxi, he had finally lost sight of them in the residential district which they now patrolled in the hope of spotting the cab.

The taxi driver was an old man with a bushy white moustache and eyebrows. He wore a blue cap and a white jacket and to Alfredo, he looked more like an old sea captain then he did a cab driver. Alfredo's eyes scanned the side streets as they passed by in the vain hope of catching a glimpse of Tom and Isabelle.

"They will be here somewhere," the taxi driver said with confidence. "They must be because there's nowhere else to go over this side of town. It's on the way to nowhere, if you don't live here or visit then there is no need to come here at all."

Alfredo could have disagreed with the old man whose accent suggested he was not a Roman, but instead he kept silent. As his eyes searched the street, he suddenly remembered his first meeting with Luca Casaraghi. Luca had dropped his wallet and his address…

"Let's take a look in Via Sicilia," Alfredo said as he leant back in the vehicle's rear seat sure in the knowledge that his hunch would prove correct.

The taxi driver turned his head and cocked an eye in Alfredo's direction. "It is just ahead on the left."

"Good, unless I'm very much mistaken we shall find what we are searching for."

Sure enough in Via Sicilia, Alfredo found the taxi. He settled his cab fare and made his way along the street to where the other taxi was parked. Opening the rear door of the cab, Alfredo climbed into the back. "I would like to go into town," Alfredo said when the taxi driver turned towards him.

"And I would like to take you," the driver responding cheerfully. "But sadly, it is impossible for I already have a fare."

"I don't see any fare," Alfredo said.

"I am waiting," said the driver, "they are collecting something from one of the apartments over there." He nodded his head in the direction of the green door. "They shouldn't be much longer, maybe you can share?"

Alfredo thanked the man and climbed from the car to make his way over to the green door. A tentative shove revealed the door to be unlocked and Alfredo stepped quietly into the darkness within. He stood in the lobby and waited for his eyes to adjust to the dimness. There was a large marble stairway to his left and to his right, a short hallway with doors leading to the ground floor apartments. Alfredo glanced up at the stairway and then back at the doors to the ground floor apartments. He listened carefully for any indication of Tom and Isabelle's whereabouts but could hear nothing.

*

Tom's eyes were fixed numbly on the pistol's barrel as Luca pulled the trigger again and again but the pistol did not fire and instead, there was only a serious of impotent clicks. Luca glared at the weapon furiously and shook it in frustration before pointing it at Tom's head again and pulling the trigger several more times.

Isabelle stood spellbound not even daring to breathe for fear that by doing so she would somehow enable Luca's pistol to fire and kill Tom, who stood paralysed by fear and seemingly unable to do anything to avert his death.

Snarling in rage, Luca whipped his arm in a backhanded blow that brought the pistol crashing into the side of Tom's face. Tom crashed to the floor, his head colliding sickeningly with the room's far wall. Luca stepped over to where Tom lay and grabbing him by his jacket collar, he lifted him to his feet before punching him savagely in the stomach. Tom folded as the breath was thrust violently from his body and Luca again brought the pistol slamming down, this time on the back of Tom's head.

Isabelle began to scream hysterically for Luca to stop as she launched herself at him and began scratching and clawing at his face and eyes. Her attack was brave and desperate but short-lived as a heavy backhanded blow from Luca sent her reeling backwards to collapse in a daze on the floor. "Wait your turn, bitch!" Luca growled before turning his attention back to Tom who lay stunned upon the floor. "This time you die, Caprietti," Luca promised as he launched a powerful kick into Tom's back.

*

Alfredo heard the screams coming from above and quickly made his way up the stairway in search of its source.

*

146

Tom's world was one of pain and confusion and he was only vaguely aware of what was going on around him. His mind wandered back to the house in which he'd grown up. He was in the bathroom washing blood from his face following a fight he'd just lost in which a larger boy had given him a sound and thorough beating. His father appeared at the bathroom door to inspect the injuries sustained by his son. The look on his father's face hurt Tom much more than the beating he'd just received.

For some reason, Tom felt the need to apologise to his father but when he tried, his pleadings were brutally brushed aside.

"Don't lose, son," his father said, "don't you ever come back to this house a loser." Dragging him to the front door, his father had pushed him out. "Now get back out there and finish the job, and this time do it properly."

*

There were three floors in the building and each had four apartments. The screaming had stopped and Alfredo didn't know where to look.

*

Tom's back arched in response to Luca's savage kick and blood sprayed from his mouth as the shock of the blow pushed Tom's teeth into his tongue and lips. Luca lifted his foot and brought the heel of his shoe slamming down at Tom's face. But this time the blow was stopped and Tom's right hand held Luca's foot just millimetres from his face. Surprised to have his attack blocked by a victim that Luca had thought was finished, he shifted all his weight to push his foot to mangle Tom's face.

Searching for something, anything to use as a defence against Luca, Tom's outstretched left hand came into contact with Luca's rack of dumbbells. His hand grabbed the metal shaft of one of the bells and with a supreme effort, Tom brought it crashing into Luca's knee cap.

Luca's agony was excruciating and he collapsed to the floor making a strange whimpered grunting noise. Tom struggled slowly to his feet to look down upon his now defenceless attacker. Blood spilled from Tom's head and mouth on to his whinging enemy.

"Shut the fuck up, you greasy fucker!" Tom growled in anger and disgust, and by doing so, sprayed Luca with blood and spittle. Luca took no notice but rocked from side to side clutching his damaged kneecap. Tom roared in anger and kicked Luca savagely in the face causing even more damage to his already broken nose. Luca cried out in pain and begged Tom to stop and take pity on him. This made Tom even angrier and he stooped down to pick up the discarded dumbbell and was about to set about Luca again when Isabelle intervened.

"Tom?"

Tom looked across the room to where Isabelle sat huddled in a corner. She had her arms around her knees which were pulled up under her chin. She looked very young, defenceless and utterly terrified. She stared at him through two large, frightened eyes.

"No more, Tom, please. I don't want to be here anymore."

Tom looked from Isabelle to Luca and back to Isabelle. He couldn't understand what she had ever seen in the man who now grovelled and whimpered at his feet. He shrugged his shoulders, such thoughts were pointless. Luca's involvement in their lives was now at an end and as soon as they left the apartment, they would never have to lay eyes on him again.

"It's finished," said Tom as he dropped the heavy dumbbell and made his way to where Isabelle sat trembling. Lifting her to her feet, they hugged each other, and Tom winced painfully when she pecked on his damaged lips. Breaking apart, Tom grabbed the battered old suitcase that was now pack full of Isabelle's belongings. "Have you got everything?" he asked.

Isabelle suddenly remembered her passport and disappeared to another room in search of it.

Left alone in the room with Luca, Tom let loose a series of quick and savage kicks at his opponent's ribs and abdomen.

"I have it now," Isabelle declared returning to the room and holding the red EU passport in her hand.

"Isabelle."

They both turned, it was Luca. He was laying curled into a foetal position and rocking back and forth in obvious agony. His face looked badly damaged and he had lost a large amount of blood from his nose. He drew a forearm across his face to wipe some of the blood away and looked pleadingly at Isabelle.

"Look, what you have done to me," he said sadly. "What did I do to deserve this? My only crime was to love you."

"What's he saying?" asked Tom, who didn't understand much Italian at all.

"Nothing," said Isabelle as she looked away from Luca to meet Tom's eyes. She turned and, with Tom following close behind, made her way towards the front door. Luca called her name again but neither of them took any notice. However, when Isabelle opened the door to leave, she jumped back in fright as she was suddenly confronted by the large form of Doctor Mido.

"Tom, Isabelle, are you all right?" he asked as he instantly took in the damage to Tom's face and head.

Alfredo did not wait for their answer or any questions they may have had but instead he pushed passed them. "Wait for me in the taxi downstairs," he said as he made his way into Luca's apartment. "I will not be long and I will explain everything."

Tom and Isabelle watched as Alfredo disappeared into the room they had just left and closed the door behind him. "Let's do as he says," said Tom and he took Isabelle's hand and led her down the stairs.

*

Luca looked up in pathetic surprise as Doctor Mido entered the room. He was about to ask the doctor what he was doing there but wasn't given the opportunity. Alfredo took in the situation in an instance. Seeing Luca's discarded weapon laying on the floor, he kicked this to one side before hauling the miserable and soundly beaten man to his feet. Luca let out a yell of pain as Alfredo pushed him back against the wall and began to search his clothing for concealed weapons.

"Doctor Mido, what are you doing?" Luca asked miserably as Alfredo continued his search. Alfredo reached inside Luca's jacket pocket and pulled out a well-padded brown envelope. Alfredo studied the name and address written neatly on the front of the envelope with interest and immediately guessed at its contents. *So the undertaker was still in business*, he thought.

"Who gave you this?" he asked Luca.

Luca looked at the envelope he taken from Franco just after he'd broken his arm. "It's mine," he said. "Why do you want to know?"

Alfredo stepped away from Luca and tapped the envelope in his big hands. "I think you're lying," he said, "you see, I know who this letter is addressed to and I do not think it's something that a police officer would be involved in."

Luca continued to follow Alfredo with his eyes as the big man stepped across to the window and peered out down to the street below. He could see that Tom and Isabelle were just leaving the building and making their way towards the taxi on the opposite side of the road.

"Probably," Alfredo continued, "you are merely looking after it for somebody else."

"What makes you think that?" Despite his pain, Luca was becoming intrigued as to what the package could actually be. So much had happened since he'd taken it from Franco that he'd forgotten all about it but now it seemed to be taking on a new significance.

"The man that this package is addressed to is a bank for certain...people," Alfredo lied as he turned back to Luca. "I know this because I once saved a man who was a big criminal and as a reward, he gave me such a package with the same name and address on the front."

Luca was following the doctor's story carefully and like the boy who followed the red balloon, he was becoming mesmerised. "I was asked to deliver the letter by hand," Alfredo continued. "I was nervous because I am not a man who mixes in such circles and so was a little afraid of what might happen but curiosity finally got the better of me and so one day, I delivered the package. Now, Mr Casaraghi, shall I take a look at your injuries?"

Luca wipe an arm across his nose and was pleased to see the bleeding appeared to have slowed. "There's no need, thanks doctor, I'm fine really, probably looks much worse than it is. Please, tell me what happened when you delivered the package?"

"Well," Alfredo said whilst making the pretence of making a cursory examination of Luca's wounded face, "I was given a substantial amount of money. It seems that I was being rewarded for saving the criminal's life. Normally I would have refused such a gift but I was young then and I didn't have much money so, I placed my morals to one side for a while and accepted what even by today's standards was a very generous gift. It was a most singular event and that is why today even after many years have passed, I still recognise the name and address of the envelope. Now how are you feeling?"

"I'm feeling much better," Luca chimed, his injuries now taking a backseat in his list of priorities. "Tell me, doctor, how did you come to be here?"

"My sister has recently moved in across the way," Alfredo lied easily, "I was paying her a visit when I heard a commotion and came to investigate. Now I will telephone the police and arrange for an ambulance. I'd feel much better if you were checked over back at the hospital."

Luca's demeanour changed suddenly as he tried to convince the doctor that these calls would not be necessary. Hopping to avoid putting weight on his damaged leg, he grabbed the doctor's arms and urged him towards the front door all the time insisting that his injuries appeared much worse than they were and that there was absolutely no need to contact the authorities. As soon as he managed to expel the doctor, Luca slammed and locked the door before hopping back to the spare room in order to retrieve the envelope that he believed would result in him claiming a fortune from the Mob's banker. Retrieving the envelope from where the doctor had placed it, Luca clutched it to his heart blissfully ignorant that what he clasped to his bosom was, in fact, the bearer's death warrant.

Chapter 30
Old Times – New Times

It was only now as she sat opposite Tom and Alfredo Caprietti that Isabelle noted for the first time their strong family resemblance. Alfredo had told them his true identity whilst they travelled in the taxi back to the hospital. Tom seemed dumbstruck by the discovery that he had a half-brother and as for Alfredo's reasons for lying about his identity, she thought her new man needed time to take in and get used to Alfredo's story together with everything else that had befallen him recently, including Isabelle herself.

Now as they sat on opposite sides of Maria's bed, Tom obediently answered questions asked by both Maria and Alfredo about Tom's late father. Tom shared whatever he knew and thought might be of possible interest to them, as well as one or two things that may have meant something to Tom but which left Maria and Alfredo looking blank.

"Tom, I am so pleased that you and your beautiful friend took the effort to find me." Maria beamed happily. "It is such a comfort for me to finally learn what became of my Alfredo. I would have given anything, anything to have seen him for one last time but perhaps it is best to stay with the memories I have. And now, God has sent you to me to tell me something about Alfredo's father." Maria smiled lovingly at her son. "And for that, I am extremely grateful! Tell me, Tom, Isabelle, what are your plans now?"

Tom looked at Isabelle for inspiration, got none, and so puffed out his cheeks and shrugged his shoulders. "I really don't know. Everything has happened so quickly that to be honest, I wouldn't mind too much if I didn't do anything for a while. At least then it would give me some time to catch up with myself if you understand what I mean."

"Most certainly," said Alfredo, "but I would recommend that you and Isabelle leave Rome before you finally relax. For some reason, the two of you seem to have attracted the wrong kind of attention and I do not believe it is altogether safe for you to stay. I could be wrong but I have never had a brother before and now that I have one, I would like to keep him safe."

"But you must leave us your contact details!" Maria put in quickly.

*

Promising to stay in contact, Tom and Isabelle exchanged hugs and kisses with Maria before leaving the hospital with Alfredo, who had insisted on escorting them back to the hotel in order to collect Tom's belongings.

At the hospital's reception desk, a smartly dressed man with one arm in plaster was sharing a joke with one of the receptionists. As they approached, he turned and stepped towards them. Alfredo immediately placed himself in front of their small group and conversed with the man in Italian.

"This man thinks you are me!" Alfredo said as he turned smiling in amusement to Tom. "He wishes your mother a swift recovery and says that you no longer have anything to fear from the Pesto family. Like I said, it's safer that you leave Rome as soon as possible."

Alfredo turned back to the stranger and they conversed for a minute or two more. Then the conversation ended and the stranger with one arm in a sling waved the other happily at Tom and Isabelle before leaving to return to the woman at the hospital's reception desk.

"He is harmless, undoubtedly, an idiot but harmless and extremely polite nonetheless." Alfredo concluded as they finally made their way out of the hospital.

*

In their hotel room, holy and birth sisters Assumptia and Magdalene Malone were just about to finish off their packing. Assumptia was gazing down lovingly at the tightly packed bundles of bank notes, which she patted gently before closing the lid of the battered old suitcase and clicking the latches shut.

"Ah it's grand to be rich!" She beamed happily as she took the case by the handle and turned to face Magdalene who, for the last ten minutes, had been waiting patiently for her sister.

"And if we want to stay rich then we must get that lot safely deposited in a bank, just as soon as we get ourselves settled." Magdalene replied as she rose to her feet and collected their other suitcase, the one that contained their meagre supply of clothing, and made her way towards the hotel door.

"Oh Maggie, we can't let a bank get hold of this! That's just foolish because they'll take just one look at the numbers on the notes and before you can say Jack Robinson, we'll be hauled off to gaol. No, we'll have to be a bit cleverer than that if we're to hold on to this lot and until we work out how we can safeguard it properly, we'll just have to watch it like hawks!"

"Do you have to shout so, Assumptia?" Magdalene moaned weakly. "My head is still pounding from all that wine we drank and my stomach is, well it's not good."

"I know what you mean," Assumptia sympathised whilst rubbing a hand over her large paunch, "I think it must have been the spicy pizza, it's playing havoc with my piles."

"Assumptia! Really, that's too much information. Now if you're finally ready, I am finding this room far too stuffy and it's making me feel quite nauseous."

*

Tom stood with his holdall across his shoulders as he scanned the checkout invoice prior to signing off the credit card receipt. He glanced over towards the door where Isabelle stood patiently beside her battered old suitcase and Alfredo mooched over the hotel's artwork.

He had arrived in Rome such a short time ago and in that time, he had found his father's lost love of sixty years earlier, a half-brother he never knew he had, and a gorgeous French girl who seemed to think the world of him.

His thoughts were disturbed as he heard people arriving behind him and he turned to see two nuns slowly approaching the counter of that part of the hotel's reception area that was dedicated to checking out. Recognising the sisters from the horrendous events at St Peter's Basilica Tom quickly turned away, whilst at the same time and for reasons unknown, reaching a hand to inspect the large bump at the top of his head. He quickly signed off the credit card receipt, bid farewell to the lady at the desk and turned to leave.

He didn't get very far as one of the nuns had placed a suitcase on the floor immediately behind where Tom stood and as he turned to leave he fell over the case and went flying across the reception area. He kicked the case in the process and this went skidding across the marble floor to where Isabelle was waiting, and the case collided with Isabelle's own which went over like a skittle hit by a bowling ball.

Seeing Tom go crashing to the floor, Isabelle left the cases and ran over to where Tom lay crumpled on the floor.

Assumptia had taken two purposeful steps towards retrieving the suitcase when she stopped short and almost doubled over. Clutching her stomach in agony and muttering something about chorizo's revenge, she quickly changed direction and made for the lavatories.

Alfredo turned and quickly assessing what had happened he tutted before reaching down and collecting one of the cases which he apologetically returned to the remaining nun.

Magdalene gazed up into Alfredo's dark eyes and felt her knees wobble. He was without a doubt the most handsome man she had ever laid eyes on and her whole body shook with new sensations as his soft voice lilted unknown Italian words at her. She could feel colour flush her cheeks and every molecule of moisture leave her mouth as she desperately tried to regain control of herself and make a fitting response to the gorgeous man.

"Oh thank you very much, you needn't nice very so kind!" she gabbled as Alfredo handed her the suitcase.

"It is a pleasure." Alfredo responded quickly converting to English. "Now, pardon me Sister, but I must now collect my family and leave. Ciao."

Magdalene stood as if transfixed as she watched Alfredo gather together the younger man and the pretty woman before leaving the hotel without so much as a backward glance.

The spell she had been placed under was not broken until Assumptia's re-emergence from the lavatory. Her portly sister stepped gingerly towards her whilst waving a hand fan-like under her nose.

"Take my advice, Maggie, and don't set foot in there! I had a bad turn and think it's trying to follow me out. Have you finished checking us out?"

"What?" Magdalene asked distractedly. "No Assumptia, I've not even began."

"Well, we'd best get a move on then." Assumptia said as she took the case from her sister's hand. "Let me pull out a wedge of notes first and then we can ask for the bill."

*

Alfredo put Isabelle and Tom on the train bound for Milan before wishing them bon voyage and good luck. They promised to get in contact again soon and waved energetically as the train slowly began to pull out, taking them on to the first stage of a journey, the final destination of which remained unknown.

Falling back into their seats, Tom let out a long sigh as Isabelle made herself comfortable under his arm.

"Are you tired, Tom?" she asked as she nuzzled into his chest.

"Very. Do you know that suitcase of yours gets heavier each time I pick it up? We were only in that apartment for five minutes. What did you do, pack the sink?"

"Tom, I think it's time you made love to me again."

Although their carriage was empty apart from the two of them, Tom was about to protest that they were nonetheless on a train and that at any moment someone might enter from another carriage. His protests died on his lips as Isabelle's head slipped down from his chest and her hands loosened his trousers.

Chapter 31

The End

Luca's car pulled to a halt outside the address written on the padded envelope. He switched on the car's internal light and checked the address again just to make sure. Pulling down the vehicle's visor Luca glanced at his reflection in the vanity mirror. He looked like he felt. He shrugged, if he received enough money he would take an extended leave, maybe even for a couple of months and relax in the sun somewhere beside the sea. He would get better in no time and then decide what he should do about certain outstanding matters. These outstanding matters included Issi, Caprietti and Franco. There were so many debts to repay but first some much needed relaxation and recovery.

Stepping painfully from the vehicle, Luca made his way over to the door of the funeral parlour. It was closed and the door was locked so Luca pressed the polished brass bell. After a short while, he heard footsteps followed by the sound of a key turning in a lock.

The door opened and standing in front of him was a tall thin man dressed all in black, which matched the deep-set circles below his sunken eyes. The man had a yellowish complexion which was accentuated by his hollow cheeks and greasy black hair.

"Hello," said Luca as he proffered the padded envelope. "I was told to deliver this to you personally."

The tall man glanced down at the envelope before taking it from Luca's outstretched hand.

"You had best come in then," the man said.

Luca stepped into the funeral parlour and the tall man closed and locked the door behind him. When the tall man turned to face Luca, his eyes were on Luca's shoes, slowly rising to the top of Luca's head.

"Six feet two?" the tall man ventured.

Luca was beginning to feel decidedly uncomfortable.

"Yes, that's accurate. A good attribute in your line of work…?"

The tall man looked at Luca solemnly, his eyes never leaving him as his fingers busied themselves opening the padded envelope. Once the envelope was open, the tall man's fingers delved inside and pulled out a folded sheet of paper, which he shook open and studied. Letting this fall slowly from his fingers the tall man prised open the envelope and scanned its remaining contents.

"It seems that you are very well thought of," the tall man said.

Luca cleared his throat nervously. He now had a very bad feeling and his senses were screaming at him to get out of his current situation as soon, and by whatever means possible. However, vying against this instinct was his greed, and his greed was fuelled by the words of the tall stranger. *Very well thought of:* could this mean that he was about to receive a very large payment?

Deciding to take the bull by the horns and put an end to this increasingly uncomfortable experience, Luca took a deep breath and said; "Would you please dispense with the formalities and give me what I came for?"